A King Production presents...

Stackin' PAPER V

Stay Schemin'...

A Novel

JOY DEJA KING

ISBN 10: 1-942217-58-7
ISBN 13: 978-1942217589
Cover concept by Joy Deja King
Cover Model: Joy Deja King

Library of Congress Cataloging-in-Publication Data;
King, Deja Joy
Stackin' Paper Part 5: a novel/by Joy Deja King

For complete Library of Congress Copyright info visit;
www.joydejaking.com Twitter: @joydejaking

A King Production
P.O. Box 912, Collierville, TN 38027

This Book is Dedicated To My:

Family, Readers, and Supporters.
I LOVE you guys so much. Please believe that!!

—Joy Deja King

"Y'all Killed X And Let Zimmerman Live
Streets Is Done..."

Jay-Z

A KING PRODUCTION
Stay Schemin'...
Stackin' PAPER V
A Novel
JOY DEJA KING

Chapter One

Bad Bitches Only

The chauffeured drop top Maybach, slowly entered the gated, private, tree-lined driveway, set back on a magnificent custom 4 acre estate with lake views all around. The majestic grounds were truly breathtaking with strategic gardens, accent fountains, annexed terraces, heated inground pool, lighted tennis court, and a gazebo overlooking a stocked pond. The exclusive residence was located in Moorestown, NJ. Though it was only 15 miles from Philadelphia, it felt like an entirely different world. The beautiful suburb seamlessly married the modern with the past.

The driver opened the back door and four women, who had the appearance of a superstar girl group, stepped out one by one. But these bad bitches didn't come to perform a chart topping Billboard single, they were hired for a much more intriguing gig.

The exquisite mahogany double doors opened and they were greeted with a, "Welcome. You can head straight to the back." The intimidatingly muscular bodyguard directed the women. After taking in the 3 story marble foyer and the grand center staircase, Shiffon, the HBIC of the group, noticed the gun toting goon, was armed with two Dan Wesson Valor 1911. But it was of no consequence to her.

"Ladies, let's go," Shiffon glanced back signaling her girls. All you heard was the clicking of their designer heels, on the Calacatta marble floor until they reached the archway.

"Well, I be muthafuckin' damned," Trae gasped, laying his playing cards down. He didn't care he'd exposed his hand. Imagining the fun he was about to have with the eye candy standing in front of him, was worth the few thousand dollars he'd inevitably lost on the card game.

"Nigga, what you doing?!" Eli, another player

at the table scoffed. It didn't take long for him and the other men in the room, to see what had garnered Trae's full attention.

"Maverick told me he had hired some prime pussy but man oh man, them hoes are exceptional," another player chimed in and said.

"Speaking of Maverick, here come that nigga now," Trae said, as he was stepping off the glass elevator.

"You already know this, but you the man, Maverick!" Eli and the other men in the room cheered.

"That must mean my special invited guests have arrived," Maverick smiled widely.

"Damn straight," Trae nodded.

"No need to stand over there. Come sit down and join us," Maverick said, walking over to the women and taking Shiffon's hand. "Would you ladies like some champagne?" he offered, pointing towards a table stocked with bottles of expensive bubbly.

"We'll be more than happy to sit down and have a drink, after you hand over our money," Shiffon stated sweetly. Although she nor the other women had any intentions of drinking.

"A woman about her business. I like that," Maverick remarked. He went over to a desk in the corner of the room, opened the drawer, retrieved some money and placed the stacks in Shiffon's hand. 'This is the amount we agreed on, plus a little extra."

"Thank you," she said, placing the money in her bag. Shiffon then turned to Essence, Bailey and Leila letting them know it was time to get to work.

The women wasted no time, taking off their Gucci G-Sequence print coats. They removed the belt on their classic silk blend trenches revealing La Perla lingerie and Dita Von Teese lace, mesh curve enhancing bodysuits.

"Gotdamn!" The men belted, seeing nothing but toned, glistening flesh.

The DJ who was hired for what was supposed to be a small birthday celebration for Klay, one of Maverick's top workers, turned the music up to get the party on ten. Cardi B's Drip featuring the Migos started blaring from the surround sound speakers, which automatically got the women hyped, to start doing what they do best... perform.

With tits and ass grinding seductively in their faces, the men were losing it. "I need you to come closer," Trae demanded, groping Bailey's thigh. His hand was itching to slide her panties to the side and get his fingers drenched in her wetness.

"What about me?" Maverick asked Shiffon with ease, while they sat watching all the pussy poppin' and lustful glares from the other side of the room.

"I was waiting for your request." Shiffon stood up, releasing her trench. As if having no impulse control, Maverick reached out and ran his hand down her bare stomach.

"You have the most beautiful skin. It's fuckin' soft too," Maverick continued, working his hand down her leg like he was mesmerized. "Why the fuck you strippin'? You supposed to be some nigga's wife."

Not replying with words, Shiffon straddled Maverick while arching her back. She placed his hands on her breasts and allowed him to cup them tightly. Unable to resist the temptation of seeing her hardened nipples, Maverick slid the lace fabric on the bra to the side. The ladies were hired to strictly dance but Shiffon had his dick so hard, he was willing to pay top dollar so they could fuck too.

"What I gotta do to have you?" Maverick moaned.

"I'm yours, daddy," Shiffon teased, before

placing her nipple in his mouth. She immediately felt his dick fighting to come out his pants. Maverick kissed, licked and sucked, gripping her waist firmly not wanting to let her go.

Shiffon caressed his face, purring and moaning, feeding into Maverick's desires. With the music blaring, intoxicated off her body, her scent, her touch, his mind was in another world, leaving him powerless.

"You have to be mine," he mumbled. It wasn't until the sharp needle pressed through his neck, did Maverick realize he had been set up.

"Genesis sent me," Shiffon whispered to Maverick, with a deadly glare in her eyes, making sure the full dosage of the clear liquid drug, trickled in his blood stream. But the first few drops were so potent, it had rendered his body paralyzed. Maverick was unable to move or speak, yet his mind was completely alert.

The notorious, yet lowkey drug kingpin, had to watch in silence as the beauty he'd instantly become infatuated with, took out his crew. Shiffon's weapon of choice was a needle for Maverick but she came with gun's blazing for his team. Eli was the first to get it. He had a bottle of champagne in one hand and gripping Leila's ass with the other. He felt zero pain as the bullet ripped through his brain.

Once Eli went down, the domino effect was in full swing. The ladies had murder on their mind and made sure to stay sober, while the men were too drunk to realize, death had shown up at the front door. Leila, Bailey and Essence retrieved guns from their trench coats, that was conveniently draped on the chair they were giving lap dances on. Trae, Klay, a couple of other men and even the DJ, who wasn't a member of Maverick's crew, were all shot dead within a matter of seconds, as Cardi B's Invasion Of Privacy continued to blast in the background.

"You all take whatever you like but keep an eye on Maverick. I'll be right back," Shiffon told her girls after checking to make sure the intended targets were deceased.

"I was wondering what was taking you so long," the muscular bodyguard who let them in said, as Shiffon walked towards him.

"I wanted time for my girl's to put on a proper show and have the liquor circulating correctly, before we put in the real work," Shiffon winked.

"Least them niggas died wit' a smile on they faces," he chuckled.

"I'm sure they did," Shiffon smirked, reaching

in her purse. "Here's your cut for staying out the way."

"Thank you," he grinned, eyeing his stacks of dead presidents.

"My pleasure. I'm about to get our driver, so he can put Maverick in the trunk. Do you wanna take your bullet in the shoulder, leg, arm....it's up to you."

"I'll take it in the arm. All these muscles will protect me," he joked.

"Cool, now hand me your guns. We want to keep this as realistic as possible. We need it to appear you were taken out. Not that you willingly let us kill everyone here and kidnap your boss."

"True," he nodded. "I already gave your driver the video footage. There's nothing to show you all coming or going," he stated, handing her his weapons.

"Perfect." Shiffon nodded, before using one of his own guns, to put two bullets in his head. "Sorry, but I can't afford to leave any witnesses," she shrugged, grabbing the money she'd just given him, from his closed fist.

Shiffon opened the front door, signaling for the driver to come inside. Her job there was done and she was ready for them to make their exit.

Chapter Two

Dead Friends

"He's moving his head. I think that means he's waking up," Nico announced. Genesis, Supreme, Lorenzo and T-Roc walked over and stood next to him. Their arms were folded becoming impatient.

"Where the fuck am I?" Maverick muttered. The echo of his voice had him thinking he was dreaming.

"You home muthafucker!" T-Roc cracked.

Maverick was still groggy from the second dosage of drugs he was given, before being dumped in the trunk and brought to his current location. He was blindfolded but his eyes were heavy and his limbs felt like wet cement on his body. "Can I get some water?" Maverick asked, feeling dehydrated.

"We ain't taking no requests right now," Nico told him.

"Yo, ya got me tied up in here. I can't see shit!" Maverick scoffed, trying to move his arms. "What the fuck is going on?" his memory was foggy but slowly he was starting to remember what happened last night. The party, the women and then Maverick put his head down. He let out a somber sigh. "Are they all dead?"

"If you're referring to your crew, then yes," Genesis replied. "They're all dead."

"Why the fuck ya didn't kill me too?"

"That can be arranged," Supreme chimed in.

"But we're willing to give you an opportunity to save yourself," Genesis said. "But only if you cooperate."

"What, this some type of ransom? You clearly know who the fuck I am! How much paper you want?"

"We don't need your money." Lorenzo was quick to let him know.

"Then what...drugs?" he questioned with

confusion.

"Maverick, we know you're partners with Arnez. You've been his main money supplier for a few years now," Supreme said. "That's a problem for us."

"You fuckin' killed members of my crew, drugged me and got me chained to this chair because of Arnez?! I got dead friends over some bullshit!" Maverick roared.

"Nigga, we gon' need you to settle down," T-Roc warned.

Genesis raised his arm, gesturing for everyone to simmer down. "I'm sure we can all sympathize with what Maverick has been through. If anything happened to one of you, I would feel some type of way too."

"Oh, so you 'bout to be on some good cop, bad cop type shit," Maverick shook his head. "You did all this bullshit for nothing. Arnez ain't my partner. I run my shit solo."

"Then explain why you've given him so much money for the last few years?" Genesis asked.

"He buys product from me like a lot of other niggas in the game."

"Save that bull..." Genesis put his hand up, before cutting Lorenzo off.

"We know about your history with Arnez.

The two of you go way back," Genesis stated.

"I don't know what you talkin' about. I'm his plug. That's it." Maverick continued his denial.

Genesis stepped forward so he was standing directly in front of Maverick. "I respect loyalty and I get why you're being loyal to Arnez right now."

"Man, you trippin'," Maverick shrugged. "My relationship with Arnez is strictly business."

"When you were a teenager, your older brother Clyde, got himself into some trouble. He crossed a rival gang member and word spread quickly he was a dead man. Your mother was friends with Arnez's mother. She begged him to save her son and he did. Arnez also put Clyde to work and got him out that gang life. Clyde eventually became a heavy hitter and when you got old enough, you started working with your brother too, until..."

"Listen, ain't no need for you to talk about my brother!" Maverick snapped, before Genesis could finish his sentence. "You don't know nothing about him."

"I know he's dead. You and your brother became partners in the drug game. Moving a lot of weight together, until he got murdered a few years ago. Whenever Arnez needed anything, your brother would come through for him. After he got killed, you took over that role. You didn't have to but you knew the loyalty Clyde had for Arnez and out of respect, you wanted to honor that."

Genesis could see Maverick's jaw flinching. His eyes were covered but that didn't stop the rage from seeping through. His muscles appeared to be throbbing against the fabric of his Givenchy denim shirt. If Maverick was confined by anything else other than chains, there was no doubt he was angry enough to break free.

He swallowed hard before finally speaking. "I can't be of no help to you." Maverick's voice was steady and his words concise.

"I see. Then I guess, I'll let you be." Genesis turned away from Maverick.

"What the fuck you doing?" Nico questioned, with the rest of the men's facial expressions asking the same thing.

"Follow me out," Genesis said, leading them to the back room in the warehouse.

"Man, if we don't start torturing that nigga to make him talk," T-Roc reasoned.

"Yeah, I'm with T-Roc on that," Lorenzo cosigned.

"I think we all are," Nico added.

"I think Genesis's decision to fall back was

the right one," Supreme spoke up and said. "He wasn't gonna break and we need him to be of sound mind. Torturing Maverick would do more harm than good."

"Didn't nobody ask you what you thought," Nico snarled.

"I don't recall anybody asking you neither but it didn't stop you," Supreme shot back."

"Fellas, let's not do this," Genesis was quick to interject, wanting to stay focused on the important shit. "Torture ain't the way to go wit' this nigga. I told you he would be difficult. He's young but keep in mind, he's seen and been through more bullshit than most have experienced in a lifetime."

"Then what's the plan?" Lorenzo asked.

"We'll have a few of our men stay with him tonight. Give him some water, let him use the restroom but no food. We'll do this for a couple days and then we'll speak to him again. I'll make sure to tell them not to drug him. Thinking about the unknown, will drive even the strongest mind crazy."

"Plus that nigga, gon' be starving. Shiiit, that nigga will be ready to tell it all for a fuckin' fry," Nico laughed.

"Let's hope because we're running out of

time," Genesis sighed. "I have to get my daughter and Skylar back home. If I don't find Arnez soon, there's no telling what that muthafucker gon' do."

Chapter Three

The Unforgivable

"Caleb, have a seat," Genesis said, closing the door behind him. "I appreciate you coming over on such short notice."

"No problem. What's going on?"

"First, I wanna thank you again for delivering Maverick to me. I hate I ever doubted you."

"Don't worry about it. I'm happy you giving me the opportunity to prove myself."

"You have nothing to prove. Business in Philly has been even more profitable since you took over for Khyree." Genesis sat on the edge of his desk, facing Caleb. "I'll admit, when Amir first suggested you handle his territory, I was skeptical but you've more than delivered."

"Have to stay on my grind. When you sleep somebody else out there workin'. But you know all this. I mean look at everything you have...this crib for one," Caleb commented glancing around Genesis's office.

"You have a lot of heart and ambition. You'll go far," Genesis reassured Caleb, patting him on the shoulder. "You remind me a lot of myself when I was your age."

"Wow! That's serious right there," Caleb grinned. "I promise, I'ma do my best not to let you down."

"I'm glad you said that because there might be something else I need you to do."

"Genesis, whatever it is, I got you. I wish I could do more. Knowing Arnez is responsible for the disappearance of your daughter and her mother, makes me sick to my stomach." Caleb glanced down at the hardwood floor, not wanting to make eye contact with Genesis. He felt this enormous guilt because of his affiliation with Arnez but Caleb was doing all he could to make it right.

"Yeah," Genesis shook his head. "Arnez has

been a thorn in my side for so many years. He's tried to destroy every person I've ever loved. It has to end..." Genesis's voice trailed off. "Maverick is the key."

"Dad, I've been calling you. Why aren't you answering your phone?" Amir stormed in the office, interrupting Genesis's and Caleb's conversation. "Caleb...I didn't realize you were in New York."

"I asked him to come." Genesis stood up.

"If you're discussing business, shouldn't I be here?" Amir questioned.

"This has nothing to do with the Philly territory. Caleb is helping me with something else."

"Something else, like what?"

Genesis ignored his son's question, directing his attention back to Caleb. "Caleb, you'll be here for the next couple days right?" Genesis wanted to confirm.

"However long you need me."

"Good. I'ma call you later on. Thanks for stopping by." Genesis shook his hand.

"Of course. It's good seeing you, Amir," Caleb stopped and said, before heading to the door. "Maybe we can go out to eat or something while I'm here."

"Sure," Amir replied flatly. "I'll call you." Amir

waited for Caleb to leave before saying another word to his father. "What's up with that?"

"Come again?" Genesis was now sitting down at his desk, looking through some papers.

"Caleb works for me, yet I come over here and the two of you are having some closed door secret meeting."

"What you meant to say, was Caleb works for me. I'm your boss. Since we've cleared that up, what can I do for you?"

"We're having some issues with one of our buyers out in LA. I think I need to go out there."

"No, you stay here. Lorenzo can handle it."

"How long is this gonna last?" Amir sat down in the chair across from his father, so Genesis would have to look at him.

"If you have something to say, then speak up because I'm busy," Genesis stated, without making eye contact with his son.

"I fucked up! How many different ways can I say I'm sorry! You won't let me handle business in LA but then you shut me down, every time I try to help bring my sister home."

"You don't have the right to call Genevieve your sister." Genesis made sure to make eye contact with Amir, when he delivered those words.

"You don't mean that."

"Oh yes the fuck I do. You a grown ass man, who put an innocent child...my child's, life in danger."

"You know I never meant for that to happen. I had no idea Arnez was even alive!"

"But yet, you saw nothing wrong with ripping her out of my life. I would still be in the dark, believing Genevieve wasn't my daughter if Arnez hadn't kidnapped her. It's the only reason you grew a conscious. What sort of sick shit is that and don't blame yo' fucked up actions on your mother."

"I've begged for your forgiveness. I'll never forgive myself. But dad, I love you and I want to make things right."

"Nothing will be right, until I bring my daughter home. And you better pray, she comes home alive. Now get the hell out my office." Genesis put his head back down, letting Amir know they had nothing left to say to each other.

Amir was ready to fall to the floor and be at his father's mercy but he knew it wouldn't garner him any sympathy. Instead, whatever if any respect, Genesis still had for his son, would further diminish. He opened his mouth to speak but instead walked out the door.

"You can't give up on your father," Talisa

said, when she saw her son walk out of Genesis's office full of defeat.

"He hates me. My own father hates me."

"Amir, don't you ever think that." Talisa took her son's hand and led him through the living room, towards the terrace, where they sat down outside. "Your father is angry but his love for you, hasn't wavered and it never will."

"You say that now but if Genevieve doesn't come home alive..." Amir's eyes watered up at the very thought of his sister being dead.

"Don't even think that." Talisa placed her hand firmly on Amir's arm.

"We all know what Arnez is capable of."

"Yes but we have to stay positive, if only to keep our sanity. Amir, you're not the only one who feels guilty. If I hadn't poured my heart out to you, you wouldn't have taken such drastic measures."

"It doesn't excuse what I did. Dad always made sure Skylar and Genevieve had around the clock security. Because of what I did, I left them vulnerable and Arnez was able to make his move."

"You have to stop blaming yourself for what Arnez did."

"How can I?!" Amir yelled. "I pray every night we find Genevieve alive but I'm scared, Mom," he admitted. "I don't think I'll be able to live with myself if she dies. Her blood will be on my hands."

Amir stared up at the sky. The sun was beginning to descend below the horizon and the light of the day was slowly fading. Amir was hoping the warm hues and the intensity of the light would be enough to calm his broken soul. But it wasn't. When Amir made the decision to permanently erase Skylar and Genevieve out of his family's life, never did he imagine, it would be the one thing that could destroy them forever.

Chapter Four

Next Move

"Yo, when you coming back to Philly?"

"Not sure yet. Depends on how long Genesis need me," Caleb told Floyd, while slouched in bed flipping through cable channels.

"Man, what about yo' birthday party? I put the deposit down at that club weeks ago. We already cancelled twice. The chick been blowing up my phone tryna find out what we doing. And you know that money nonrefundable."

"Fuck that deposit!" Caleb scoffed.

"You eighteen now. We gotta celebrate that

shit!" Floyd insisted.

"I can't think about celebrating right now. After I get my business handled wit' Genesis, then we can party."

"You too young to be workin' all the fuckin' time. You don't never wanna have no fun," Floyd complained. "What business you got going on wit' that man anyway? You been mad secretive."

"Just a new connect he might want me to deal with," Caleb lied. Floyd was like his family but Genesis was adamant not to discuss his daughter's kidnapping with anybody. Caleb had too much respect for his boss, not to obey his request. "Let me call you back."

"Why?" Floyd asked, pissed Caleb was trying to end their conversation.

"Cause somebody keep calling on the other line and I wanna know who the fuck it is."

"What number is it?"

"Man, you ask more questions than a fuckin' worrisome ass broad. It say unknown. I'll hit you back," Caleb said clicking over. "Yo, who this?"

"I was beginning to think I wouldn't get you on the phone."

"I should be saying that shit to you." Caleb's once relaxed posture was now sitting in an upright position. He hadn't heard from Arnez and was relieved they finally were in contact. "Where you been? Your phone been going straight to voicemail. I couldn't even leave no more messages...that shit was full."

"I have business to deal with. I couldn't be disturbed. Where are you?"

Before answering, Caleb debated if he should tell Arnez the truth. "I'm in New York."

"What you doing there?"

"Amir wanted to meet with me. He's thinking about having me expand outside of Philly. Wanted us to meet with potential connects." Caleb was making up the lie as he went along but it sounded legit. "That's the reason I was tryna get in touch with you. Wanted to get yo' input on what I should tell Amir."

"I'm done wit' that other number. No need to call it anymore. Has Amir mentioned anything else to you, since you've been there?"

"Nope." Caleb was about one hundred percent positive Arnez was alluding to the kidnapping. But he wanted to keep mum on the subject and allow him to bring up the topic. Caleb knew Arnez was suspicious by nature and had to proceed with caution.

"Have you concluded your dealings with Amir?"

"Not yet. Probably be here for the next couple days."

"Find a way to get missing. I need to speak with you…in person."

"It can't wait?"

"If it could, we wouldn't be on the phone. I'ma call you back in about an hour with the address to where I want you to meet me. Answer."

Arnez hung up without giving Caleb the slightest opportunity to respond, which only meant this meeting was mandatory. Caleb wasn't sure how he should proceed. He'd planned on killing Arnez the night Mack and his crew was taken out but when he got to Arnez's crib, he had vanished. A couple days later he got word Genevieve and Skylar had been kidnapped and Arnez was responsible. Now Caleb needed Arnez to stay alive, at least until Genesis' daughter and the mother of his child were safe.

"Fuck!" Caleb barked, tossing the television remote across the bed. "Genesis ready to set the streets on fire to find Arnez and I'm 'bout to be up in that nigga's face. Maybe it's time for me to come clean," Caleb said out loud, reaching for his phone before hesitating.

If Genesis finds out I've been working with Arnez, I'm fuckin' dead. Ain't no coming back from that. Genesis will feel it's the ultimate betrayal, even if my loyalty has always been to him. How can I get rid of Arnez but also help Genesis get his family back without linking myself to the enemy? I gotta figure this shit out, Caleb thought to himself as he waited for Arnez's call.

$$$

"How you feeling...you comfortable?" Genesis questioned, taking a seat across from Maverick.

"I'm chained to a chair. How the fuck you think I feel," he shrugged. "All I've had is some water. How long you plan to starve a nigga?" Maverick spit.

"My man, that's all up to you." Genesis gave a casual reply, folding his hands.

"I ain't yo' man and ain't shit up to me. If it was, you wouldn't be sittin' there and I wouldn't be held captive in this dreary ass warehouse," Maverick huffed. "And oh yeah, thanks for taking the blindfolds off but I guess I need to be able see, so I can piss straight," he cracked.

Genesis let out a slight laugh. "You haven't had food in a few days. Your living conditions ain't nothing nice, yet your rage is helping you maintain your strength. Very impressive."

"Let's cut through all this bullshit. I'ma dead man. The minute I let them chicks through my front door, the clock started ticking on my life. The only reason you ain't killed me yet, is because you think you need me. I done seen yo' face. I know yo' name and who you are. You always planned on killin' me. So stop actin' like, we 'bout to do business together and if I help you, then you'll help me." Maverick pierced his eyes at Genesis with a stone cold stare on his face.

"I'm disappointed," Genesis stood up and said. "If we had met under different circumstances, we coulda made major money together. You got a lot of heart. These new breeds of so called drug kingpins, lack that. There is no need to make this harder than it has to be. Tell me where Arnez is."

"You need to pick up that gun," Maverick said, eyeing the weapon on the table, next to where Genesis was standing. "And put a bullet right in my head, cause I ain't no snitch and I ain't tellin' you shit."

Genesis gave Maverick a haunting glare. He was trying to look deep inside to get a read on his detainee. He needed to know if he was simply poppin' big shit, or if Maverick truly meant it. Unfortunately, Genesis quickly realized, the man chained up in front of him, meant every single word.

"Then we'll do things your way," Genesis stated confidently, leaving Maverick pondering what would be his next move.

Chapter Five

Shattered

"I missed waking up in your arms." Precious turned over in bed and whispered in Supreme's ear.

"It's nice to finally have my wife back home." Supreme pulled Precious in closer, kissing her on the forehead. "But I'm glad you stayed in Miami with Aaliyah."

"Me too," she grinned. "I accomplished everything I needed to get done and my motherly duties are done. Well, at least for the moment," Precious laughed. "But hopefully, Aaliyah won't be encountering anything of this magnitude ever again."

"Yeah, I think this nonstop chaos is starting to wear on all of us."

"I guess that means the situation with Genesis hasn't gotten better?" Precious adjusted the sheet over her naked body, sitting up in bed. "You still haven't told me what happened."

"With everything going on with Aaliyah, I didn't want you dealing with any additional stress."

"I'ma big girl. You know it takes a lot to stress me out."

"Trust me, I'm well aware of that," Supreme smiled, moving a strand of hair from over her eye. "I know you tough, doesn't mean I don't worry about you."

"I think that's so sweet. It makes me love you more than I already do, if that's even possible." Precious leaned in and kissed Supreme. "But no need to worry about me, all is well. Aaliyah and Dale have reunited and are back in love. Our daughter has finally gotten her happy ending. We can rejoice."

"Aaliyah's happiness is always most important to me but I still have my reservations about Dale," Supreme sighed. "He was ready to take all of us out. We can't dismiss that."

"I'm not dismissing anything. Dale is aware he's on my watchlist and this was his one and only do over. But I truly believe he's in love with Aaliyah and grateful he's been giving a second chance to make things right. And soon, they'll also be welcoming a child into this world. Dale won't fuck up again."

"He bet not," Supreme nodded.

"I love how protective you are, over me and Aaliyah just everyone you care about...even Genesis." Precious lovingly stroked Supreme's hand. "So please, tell me what's going on with him. I've been away so long, I feel completely out the loop," Precious shook her head.

Supreme allowed Precious to keep rambling, as he had no interest in discussing what was going on with Genesis. But now that his wife was home, the conversation was inevitable.

"Speaking of being out the loop, I need to call Skylar. I've been completely fixated with this Aaliyah dilemma. Gosh, I must seem like the worst Godmother ever. I'ma text Skylar right now and see if she wants to have a late lunch or dinner tonight," Precious said, reaching for her phone.

"Don't do that," Supreme interjected, placing his hand over her phone.

Precious frowned her face at Supreme. "I get you all are pissed Skylar lied about Genevieve's paternity and men like to stick together, when it's convenient for their cause," Precious sniped sarcastically. "But she's still my friend and Genevieve is my Goddaughter. My relationship with them hasn't changed." Precious politely removed Supreme's hand from over her phone to continue with her text message.

"Skylar, isn't gonna reply to your text."

"Excuse me?! Why would you say something like that?"

"Arnez is alive and he kidnapped Skylar and Genevieve."

"Not the baby!" Precious closed her eyes in despair. "That sick muthafucker refuses to die! Then he's putting an innocent child's life in danger. His dumbass don't even realize Genevieve isn't Genesis's daughter. We have to do something, Supreme! I know Genesis is still furious over Skylar's deceit and he has every right to be. But we can't let Arnez harm Skylar and Genevieve. Dear God, please don't let them be dead," Precious pleaded.

"Calm down. That's why I didn't want to tell you what was going on." Supreme got up from the bed."

"Genevieve is my Goddaughter and Skylar is my friend. How dare you keep this from me! You know how much I adore that little baby."

"I know but..."

"But what? Just say it, Supreme!"

"Genesis is doing everything humanly possible to bring Genevieve and Skylar home."

"I find that hard to believe under the circumstances," Precious sneered.

"The circumstances have changed. Genevieve is his daughter."

"Huh...what? Now I'm confused. They did a paternity test and Genesis wasn't the father. Skylar was damn near ready to slit her wrist behind that shit. She was inconsolable."

"The paternity test was switched. Genesis is the father."

"What!" Precious' eyes widened. "Who in the hell would do some foul shit like that...not Talisa? I know she don't care for Skylar but she wouldn't rip out Genesis's heart like that," Precious reasoned. "But who..."

"Amir." Supreme finally revealed.

"Are you serious!" Precious shook her head in disbelief. "If something happens to his daughter, Genesis will never forgive him. Amir better pray Genevieve is found alive."

$$$

"T-Roc, it's good to see you. I didn't realize you were here," Amir said, reaching out to shake his hand.

"Yeah, I had to meet with your dad. He wanted to discuss a few things with me before I head to Miami."

"Miami. Are you going there to see Justina?" Amir questioned.

"It's a business trip but I'm hoping to see her, while I'm there," T-Roc explained.

"How's she doing?"

"She seems to be doing very well. Not sure if you heard but Justina recently got married and they're expecting a baby."

Amir felt his heart drop. Hearing those words was a complete blow. It wasn't until that very moment, he grasped how deep his feelings still ran for his ex. "Married...baby...it feels like we only broke up yesterday," he mumbled, completely baffled.

"I'll admit, I was surprised too. It all seemed so sudden but my little girl says she's happy. That's all a father can ask for."

"Desmond." Amir paused as if unable to

bring himself to ask the question. "Is the man she married named Desmond."

"That's him," T-Roc nodded. "Desmond Blackwell."

Amir felt a rush of heat engulf his body. He took off his jacket and unbuttoned his shirt, feeling like he couldn't breathe and needed air.

"Are you okay?" T-Roc asked, seeing the distress in Amir's face.

"Yeah, I'll be alright. I guess I'm not over your daughter yet," Amir admitted.

"It doesn't feel good does it."

"Not sure what you mean?" Amir seemed puzzled.

"I remember how devastated Justina was, when she found out you and Aaliyah were seeing each other behind her back. She was crushed. So whatever you're feeling, it was a hundred times harder on my daughter."

"T-Roc, you know how horrible I felt about hurting Justina but we moved past it. I thought I was gonna marry your daughter. I was in love with her...I still am."

"It's too late now. Justina's married and has moved on. I suggest you do the same." T-Roc patted Amir on the shoulder and walked out the door.

"I thought I heard voices out here," Genesis said coming out his office. "Were you talking to someone?"

"I ran into T-Roc as he was leaving out. We had an interesting conversation."

"What did he say because you don't look too good?" Genesis asked due to the traumatized expression on his son's face.

Amir was staring down at the hardwood floor, repeating in his head every word T-Roc said, before glancing up to answer his father's question. "Justina got married."

"Really? I didn't even know the two of you broke up."

"It happened while I was in Miami for Aaliyah's wedding. I didn't have a chance to tell you because you know, everything that's been going on with Arnez."

"I see." Genesis's terse, two word reply only pushed Amir to reveal more.

"Justina's also pregnant. I know she was seeing this guy while we were together but it all seems so sudden for her to be married and pregnant." Amir's forehead creased up as in deep thought. "I can't help but wonder..." His voice trailed off.

"Wonder what?" Genesis was curious to know.

"'If there's a possibility, the baby she's carrying is mine."

"Why would you think that?"

"Because we've been together several times over the last few months. I don't know when their relationship started but there had to be a lot of overlapping," Amir reasoned.

"Or maybe, Justina only recently got pregnant and shared the news with T-Roc, as soon as she found out," Genesis said, giving another plausible explanation.

"I guess but I need to know for sure."

"Then why don't you ask her," Genesis suggested.

"Maybe I should but dad, what if Justina doesn't tell me the truth? I'm positive, she has her new husband believing the baby is his. Why would she admit otherwise and mess up this new life she's created?"

"You believe Justina would knowingly keep you away from a baby that could be yours?"

Amir stared up at the coffered ceiling with frustration. "I don't know!" he shook his head. "But if Justina is carrying my child, married or not, she won't keep me from my baby," Amir vowed.

"But yet you had no problem, keeping me from mine," Genesis stated.

Amir froze, taken aback by his father's words. There was a painful knot in his stomach. It felt worse than any punch.

"Dad!" Amir called out but Genesis had escaped back to his office and shut the door.

Chapter Six

Vicious

When the dark tinted SUV pulled into the garage, Caleb couldn't help but wonder if this was where Arnez had Skylar and Genevieve stashed. The drive to the house on the outskirts of New York City was somewhat long and unmemorable. Caleb was trying his best to remember every street and each turn but the driver had taken him on the scenic route, which he figured was no accident. Not only that, it was pitch black outside, so Caleb felt like he was lost in the woods somewhere.

"Are you gonna unlock the door or what?"

Caleb scoffed when the driver turned off the ignition.

"Arnez wants us to wait here for a few minutes," the driver said, eyeing Caleb through the rearview mirror.

Yo is this some type of setup?! Is this nigga Arnez about to kill me! Fuck! I'm out here in the middle of nowhere. Don't nobody know where I'm at. If I die tonight, my family probably won't never find my body to give me a proper burial, Caleb thought to himself.

"Man, I ain't got time to be sittin' here all night. If Arnez got other shit to do, we can speak later. All this waitin' ain't cool," Caleb complained. "And why the fuck can't I unlock this fuckin' door?!" he barked, banging on the window.

"Why all the hostility?" Arnez seemed to appear like a ghost. "Are you getting out?" he asked, holding the passenger door open.

Caleb hesitated. He was beginning to think his mind was playing tricks on him. *Calm the fuck down, Caleb. This ain't the time to show weakness. Put yo' game face on and stick to the plan!* He screamed to himself.

"I told you I was in New York for some business with Amir. If I go missing for too long, that nigga gon' get suspicious. Neither of us want that."

"Then you better get out the car, so we can talk." Arnez clapped his hands, giving Amir his signature devilish grin.

Caleb followed Arnez up the stairs and through a door that led to a spacious two level house. Caleb's eyes darted around the room, searching for any signs that a baby might be there.

"Why you staying way out here?" Caleb asked casually, as Arnez led him down the hall, to a room in the back.

"Can I get you something to drink?" Arnez offered, opening a mini refrigerator by the bar. "Have a seat. Get comfortable."

"I'll take a bottle water," Caleb said, sitting down on the sectional couch, putting his long legs on the ottoman. "You said get comfortable," he laughed.

"Yes, I did and you definitely have," Arnez smiled, handing Caleb the bottle.

Caleb could see Arnez's demeanor shifting. With him acting more relaxed, it allowed Arnez to feel at ease to put his guard down.

"When I didn't hear back from you the other night, I figured you were in disappearing mode again," Caleb said, taking a few sips of water.

"My intentions was to call you back in an

hour but I have a lot going on right now. How's business in Philly?"

"It's coming. Things are pretty hectic in the streets. I haven't spoken to you since it happened but I'm sure you heard about Delondo."

"Yeah, I did."

"You mentioned wanting to get rid of him. Did you have anything to do wit' that?" Caleb asked, although him and Floyd had assumed it was actually Astrid, Delondo's wife.

"No but I wish I had. Maybe if I acted sooner, my sister would be alive."

"So that was your sister found dead with him," Caleb shook his head, pretending to be shocked. "I know you said she was supposed to be leaving town. I was hoping that was somebody else."

"What happened to Astrid is a good example of waiting too long to make your move. If I had insisted she leave town sooner, my sister would be alive today," Arnez said with sadness filling his voice.

"Man, I'm sorry about your sister, I really am," Caleb said, thinking back to that night, when Floyd put a bullet through Astrid's chest trying to protect him.

"Me too but whoever killed my sister, will

meet the same fate but right now I have more pressing issues. It's the reason I needed to see you." Arnez lit a Newport before continuing. Caleb couldn't help but zoom in at the scarring on Arnez's left hand. It would be a forever reminder from when Maya burned down the house, leaving him for dead. The stiff, discolored skin seemed painful, even though it had healed long ago.

"What's the pressing issue?"

"A very close business associate of mine is missing. His name is Maverick."

"I've never heard you mention him before."

"I like to think of Maverick as my secret weapon. He's the reason I've been able to fund this entire operation." Arnez took another pull from his cigarette. "But clearly, he's no longer a secret."

"You think someone took him because of his affiliation with you?"

"Yes," Arnez nodded. "And I'm almost positive Genesis is behind it."

"Really?" Caleb wasn't sure if Arnez was suspicious of him and dissecting his reaction, so he felt it best to just play it cool.

"Yes. That's why I asked if Amir mentioned anything to you."

"No, he hasn't. From what you told me, don't

them niggas think you dead?"

With force and frustration Arnez put out his cigarette in an astray that was halfway filled, before immediately lighting up another one. *Boy oh boy, this nigga stressed,* Caleb thought to himself.

"Yes but things have changed."

"What things?"

"Nothing I wanna discuss with you right now," Arnez said abruptly. "I need you to find out if Genesis has Maverick and his location."

"I'll do the best I can but if what you sayin' is true, don't you think Genesis would've had this dude Maverick killed by now?"

"No because as far as Genesis is concerned, Maverick is the only link to finding me. But he won't be of any use," Arnez scoffed.

"Why you say that?"

"He'll never tell Genesis anything about me." Arnez stated with unwavering confidence.

"You sound awfully sure of yourself."

"I am. Maverick is everything I envision you'll eventually be."

"Which is?"

"A warrior. That's why I need you to find him. Men like Maverick are a dying breed in these streets. I'm not worried about him turning on me. But without his money and connections, this operation I'm trying to maintain won't survive," Arnez admitted.

"I'll do the best I can."

"I need you to do better than that! It took a very precise, executed plan, to gain access to a man like Maverick. He is always very well protected. It would take someone with a lot of resources to pull this off. This has Genesis written all over it. You're close to Amir which means you have a direct line to his father...utilize it."

"Arnez, if you're right and Genesis does have Maverick. I'll find out where he is and let you know. I can see this shit got you stressed but I don't think all that smoking back to back is beneficial to yo' health."

"Let me worry about my health and you focus on finding Maverick. I need him back home...you understand?"

Caleb recognized the sinister tone in Arnez's voice. It was more prominent when he seemed to be on edge. "I understand. I better get back to the city. For what you need, it's most important I stay on good terms with Amir."

"Yes it is. I need for you to work fast on this. I don't have much time," Arnez stood up and said, as Caleb was about to walk out.

"I'm on it...but umm, you never told me why Genesis now thinks you're alive," Caleb mentioned casually, taking a final sip of his water.

"Let's just say, I've taken something very valuable to him."

"Do you have any intentions of giving it back?" Caleb threw the question out there, as if he didn't know this valuable thing Arnez cited, was Genesis's beloved daughter.

"Of course not...never," Arnez winked.

$$$

Shiffon was on her way out of town, when she received the phone call from Caleb, that her services were needed. Initially, she turned it down, due to the new gig she was hired for. But once he said Genesis offered to pay double than her previous assignment, she willingly took the assignment.

"Are you ready?" Shiffon asked Essence who was sitting shotgun.

"Bitch, you know I'm always ready," Essence smiled, showing off the perfect set of teeth, she spent a grip on.

"Then let's do this." Shiffon returned the smile as the dynamic duo headed to the front door.

"I'll knock!" Essence offered with enthusiasm.

"Go right ahead. All I want is someone to open the door. Fuck how we get it done."

The women could hear someone walking towards the door and then quiet movement as they approached. They figured, the person on the other side of the door, was checking through the peephole to see who the unexpected guests were.

"Can I help you with something?" the well preserved woman in her mid-fifties asked.

"I'm Officer Jenkins and this is Officer Patterson. We're from the Asbury Park Police Department." Shiffon stated, flashing their fraudulent badges. The woman hesitated for a moment. She had never seen two young black females, in police uniform together at the same damn time before. But the ladies looked legit, so she put her apprehension to the side and chose to fully cooperate.

"What can I do for you officer?" the woman asked.

"Earlier today, someone came into our precinct and filed a missing person's report for a Maverick Channing."

"That's my son!" The woman gasped, putting

her hand against her chest."

"Yes, we're aware of that. Your name was listed on the report."

"It's the reason we came to speak with you," Essence added.

"I haven't heard from him in a couple days but I figured he was traveling. Are you saying something happened to my son?" her voice cracked.

"We're not sure. But a body was discovered this morning, fitting the description on the missing person report. We were hoping you could come down and identify the body. See if it's your son," Shiffon said.

"Dear God No! Not my baby!" She wailed, leaning forward.

"Do you need to sit down? Let me help you," Shiffon offered, holding the woman up so she didn't fall.

"Thank you but I'm fine. Let me get my purse and keys. I can follow you all in my car."

"No!" Essence shouted.

Shiffon cut her eyes at Essence letting her know to shut the fuck up. The woman also seemed startled by Essence's outburst.

"Please excuse Officer Patterson. Recently a father of two lost his life, after he decided to follow us in his own car. It was obvious to us he was in no condition to drive but we allowed him to do so. Unfortunately he got into a fatal car accident. Officer Patterson is still harboring some guilt," Shiffon explained.

"Oh, I see," the woman swallowed hard, taking in what Shiffon said.

"Under the circumstances, why don't you ride with us," Shiffon suggested. "We would hate for anything bad to happen to you."

"Thank you so much. Let me get my purse. I'll be right back," she said, wiping away a tear.

"Sorry about that," Essence whispered when the woman disappeared to the back. "When she said she was gonna drive herself, I freaked out. I'm so sorry!"

"I handled it," Shiffon snapped, putting an end to her whining. "Just keep your mouth shut. I'll take it from here."

"I'm ready," the woman came out and said, clutching her purse.

"Then we better get going," Shiffon smiled. "For your sake, I hope the man at the morgue isn't your son."

"I appreciate you saying that young lady...I mean officer," she said nervously.

"It's okay. I know this is difficult for you and

call me Kim."

"You're so sweet. Thank you, Kim."

Shiffon took the unsuspecting woman's hand and led her out the door to the awaiting car. It was almost frightening how she was able to transform into anyone she needed to be with such ease. It was also the reason Shiffon was one of the best assassins in the business.

Chapter Seven

Never Coming Home Again

When Caleb got back to his hotel room, he immediately got on his laptop. Within seconds he was able to listen to everything going on around Arnez. He was still in the same room Caleb had only left a couple hours ago. He could hear the television but Caleb was praying he would be hearing baby news sooner rather than later.

After Arnez didn't immediately call back within an hour like he stated, Caleb took advantage of the extra time. He reached out to one of his gadget geek associates and got his hands on an Amber Alert GPS Smart Locator. It was a tiny device coming in at 1.77 x 1.68 x .78. The durable, small GPS tracking device provided real time updates on a child's location at all times. Due to its size, you could easily conceal it in a child's pocket, coat or backpack without it being easily detectable. Caleb wasn't able to put the device on Arnez, so he instead left it hidden in between a cushion on the sectional. There was one serious downside. The battery life was only 40 hours. That would be fine if you knew your child was coming right back home but Caleb was trying to find a child, so the clock was ticking quickly.

Caleb knew it was a long shot but very much worth the gamble. In his gut, he felt it wasn't an accident Arnez was staying in a house out in the middle of nowhere. It would literally take a GPS device to find the location. The ideal spot to hide a baby, especially on a long term basis. Now all Caleb could do is stay glued to his laptop and wait.

$$$

"I see you back," Maverick frowned up his face at

Genesis and said. "Ain't shit changed," he shrugged. "So, unless you came to ask what I'd like for my last meal, we ain't got nothin' to discuss."

"The more I learn about you, the more respect I have. You really are married to this game," Genesis nodded.

"What tha fuck you mean by that?" Maverick thought Genesis's comment came out of left field, which sparked his curiosity.

"You have no wife or a significant other. No children. You're not emotionally tied to anyone. It's a golden rule to the game, that very few abide by. It's also the downfall for most of us. Loved ones are our weakness which always makes them a target. You've found a way to divert that target. I think because I was ripped from my family at a very young age, instead of running away from love, I ran towards it."

"Why are you telling me this?" Maverick questioned, becoming uneasy with where their conversation was going.

"Because no matter how fast you run from love, we all come from a woman," Genesis stated.

Maverick's jaw began to flinch and he bit down on the inner skin of his mouth. "Muthafucka, you lucky I'm chained to this chair because I would kill you wit' my bare hands," he threatened and Genesis believed him too. Maverick was the very opposite of dumb and he knew exactly what was coming next. The only question was how far had it gone. In less than sixty seconds he knew.

"Your mother seems to be very sweet," Genesis smiled, turning on a television screen with a live feed of Maverick's mother. She was bound and gagged in what appeared to be the same type of dusty warehouse as him.

"You has got to be the foulest nigga I done ever came across in my life!" Maverick growled. "Mother's supposed to be off limits. You a fuckin' animal."

"Everything you said is facts," Genesis agreed. "For my family, I am an animal."

"You would really kill my mother?!" there was no hiding Maverick's astonishment.

"To get my daughter back, not only will I kill your mother, I will let you watch, while she is tortured for days. Your mother's pain will be so agonizing, she'll be begging to die but we won't kill her. The torment will continue until she's so weak, her pleas can no longer be heard. Right when she's on the brink of death, we'll bring her back to life and start the process all over again."

"You sick FUCK!!!!!!!!!!!! AHHHHHHHHHH!!!!" Maverick's rage roared throughout the building. Genesis was finally staring in the eyes of a broken man. He was beginning to believe it would be impossible. Maverick proved to be a much tougher opponent than he anticipated.

"Is protecting Arnez worth your mother's life? If it is, then so be it. Let the torture begin." Genesis's declaration was cold and calculated. Heartless wasn't a strong enough word to describe his demeanor.

"You've crossed the line."

"No, I'm simply creating a new line. Arnez is the one who crossed it, when he took my daughter and the mother of my child. Now, I've wasted enough time and I've lost my patience with you. What's it gonna be Maverick, your mother or Arnez?"

$$$

"Do we have our men in place?" Lorenzo questioned Nico, who seemed to be preoccupied with an article he was reading in the newspaper.

"Yes but I'm sure it's a waste of time. Genesis won't get that unregenerate ass nigga to crack," Nico sneered.

"You really should have more faith, Nico," Supreme countered, walking into the office, catching both men off guard.

"What the hell are you doing here? This is our office," Nico sulked.

"I know. Mine is much bigger but that's beside the point," Supreme countered with amusement. "Good news, we have Maverick's mother."

"Get the fuck outta here," Nico snarled, tossing down his paper.

"You sure?" Lorenzo didn't sound convinced. "Last we heard, Genesis couldn't even verify an address for her."

"Because there wasn't one. The house where she lives, is listed under some corporation Maverick owns. It took some digging but we figured it out," Supreme explained.

"Does Maverick know yet?" Nico asked.

"If he doesn't, I'm sure he will very soon."

"That nigga determined to be so hard. If his mother can't break him then nothing will," Lorenzo rationalized.

"True but I think we're in a much better position. They seem to be close. He has his mother living very well. I don't see Maverick letting his mother die to save Arnez." Supreme told Lorenzo and Nico.

"You better be right because I don't have a good feeling about this. Arnez hasn't made any further contact with Genesis in two weeks now. It makes me think..." Nico's voice faded out.

"Makes you think what?" Lorenzo wanted to know.

"Don't even say it!" Supreme barked.

"Don't stand there and act like you ain't thought it too!" Nico fumed, pointing his finger at Supreme. "You too, Lorenzo. Maybe, neither one of you want to admit it but we all know what Arnez is capable of. He's a sadistic monster. None of us would be surprised if Skylar and Genevieve are already dead."

Lorenzo pulled out a chair from underneath the conference table and sat down. Supreme was standing in front of the massive window, looking out at the view of the Brooklyn Bridge. Nico was now standing up with his hands firmly in his pockets. The stillness, allowed each of them to become lost in their private thoughts.

"I still mourn for the death of my unborn child," Supreme said, resting his eyes on Nico for a moment before continuing. "So, I can only imagine how grief stricken Genesis will be if for whatever reason, we can't bring Genevieve home alive. God forbid if that does happen, we all have to be there for him. Genesis won't survive if we're not."

"And what about Amir," Lorenzo shook his head. "He'll be plagued with guilt for the rest of his life."

"As he should be!" Nico shouted. "Amir has ruined his relationship with his father and he has no one to blame but himself," he added.

"True but if we can bring Genevieve home, it might take some time but I believe the two of them can reconcile. That's his son and Genesis loves him," Lorenzo said.

"I agree. We have to remain optimistic. Hopefully at this very moment, Maverick is telling Genesis where we can find Arnez. I refuse to let my mind go to a dark place and think any other way," Supreme insisted, as he stared back out the window, saying a silent prayer for Skylar and Genevieve.

Chapter Eight

Selfish Acts

For the last hour, Amir had been in his apartment, pacing back and forth, debating whether or not he should call Justina. Ever since T-Roc told him about her pregnancy, he had so many questions. Amir tried to put them out of his mind but he couldn't let it go. Finally, he realized there would be no silencing the voices in his head, until speaking to his ex.

"Hello."

"Hey, Justina. It's me Amir."

"Hi." There was an awkward quietness before

she continued to speak. "I didn't recognize your number."

"Yeah, I changed it a few weeks ago. It's probably a good thing because I doubt you would've answered if you knew it was me."

"That's not true. I don't have any ill feelings against you. I figured you were the one who hated me."

"I ain't gon' lie, I was pretty pissed off the last time I saw you. Finding out I was being dumped for another man, when I came to pick you up at the hospital, wasn't ideal."

"I'm sorry about that. It wasn't how I planned to tell you. It was never my intention to hurt you," Justina told him.

"Honestly, I don't wanna rehash that. I called about something else."

"What is it?"

"I ran into your father the other day. He told me you got married."

"Really...I'm surprised he told you."

"I think what's more surprising is how quickly it happened. We haven't even been broken up that long."

"True but after Desmond almost died, we decided life is too short and unpredictable, so why wait."

"I see. So the quick wedding had nothing to do with your pregnancy?" Amir asked.

"I see my father was in a very talkative mood the day you saw him," Justina replied sarcastically. "And to answer your question, no that isn't the reason we got married so soon. We're in love, Amir. We didn't feel the need to wait."

"Is there a chance the baby is mine, Justina?" Amir decided to cut through the bullshit and ask the hard question.

"Excuse me?!" she sounded stunned but Amir pressed on.

"How far along are you? We were still having sex Justina so unless you're only a month or two pregnant, there's a chance the baby is mine... right?"

"Wrong. I'm only six weeks pregnant. I only found out recently and shared the news with my dad. I wasn't expecting him to spread the news. So no!" Justina yelled, "This baby isn't yours. My husband, Desmond is the father."

"Something about this doesn't feel right to me."

"That's your problem, Amir. Listen, I have to go and please don't call me again."

Before Amir could utter another word, Justina had hung up. He was about to call her right back but he heard someone knocking at the door. Amir was cursing Justina out, as he went to see who was there. When he looked through the peephole, Amir was shocked to see the familiar face.

"Precious, what a pleasant surprise. How are you?"

"I'm fine and you?"

"So, so but please come on in," Amir said, moving to the side to clear the entrance.

"Your doorman wasn't at the front desk, so I just came up. Hope you don't mind," Precious smiled.

"Of course not. Can I get you something to drink?" Amir offered.

"No, I'm good."

"When did you get back? Last I heard you were still in Miami with Aaliyah."

"About a week ago," she said, sitting down in the living room.

"I take it everything must be good with Aaliyah then. I know you wouldn't leave unless it was."

"Yes, she's back with Dale and all seems to be going smoothly. I wouldn't be surprised if they're already planning another wedding."

"If I get an invite, I'll probably pass on that. I

think we're all still recuperating from the drama at the first one," Amir cracked.

"Yes, especially with all the drama currently going on which you played a major part in. I'm so disappointed in you. What were you thinking, Amir, having the paternity results switched?"

"I wasn't thinking." Amir put his head down as the shame crept up.

"Do you have any idea the damage you've caused. Your sister and Skylar might be dead because of you."

"No! You can't put that on me. Arnez is the reason they're missing!" Amir shot back

"Genesis had round the clock security for them, until he got the results of the paternity test, saying he wasn't the father. You did that!" Precious snapped, pointing her long almond shaped nail in Amir's face. "Arnez wouldn't have been able to get to them."

"We don't know that for sure! Arnez is so fuckin' twisted. He's capable of anything!" Amir stood up from the couch, frustrated. "This is Arnez's fault not mine!"

"Keep telling yourself that," Precious countered. "All the stupid things for you to do, Amir," she sighed. "I just don't understand why you did it. It can't be due to sibling rivalry," Precious rolled her eyes. “So, what were you trying to accomplish? I can’t wrap my mind around it.”

“I’m sick about Skylar and Genevieve but no one understands how hard this entire situation has been for my mother. She tried to appear like she was okay with everything but I saw the pain in her eyes. My mother didn’t deserve that. She had already been through so much. She never even got the chance to hold me when I was a baby. Then here comes Skylar, living the life my mother was robbed of. It wasn’t fair.”

“And you think letting Skylar and Genevieve get kidnapped is?”

“I didn’t even know Arnez was alive! Never, not even in my worst nightmare did I want or think this would happen.”

“I believe you but what about ripping a father away from his child. You were willing to let Genesis think Genevieve wasn’t his daughter. Do you know how devastated Skylar was.”

“Call me selfish but I was only worried about my own mother’s devastation,” Amir conceded. “With that being said, I do understand how callous my actions were,” he acknowledged. “Especially now.”

“Why now?” Precious questioned.

Amir let out a deep sigh and glanced over at a

framed photo of his mother and father he placed on the built-in bookshelf. They looked happy and in his heart, that's all he wanted for his parents. He now wondered if it was even a possibility.

"The why now, comes from a situation I'm currently dealing with," Amir said, while walking back over to sit down next to Precious. "Justina probably hasn't shared the news, so please keep what I'm about to tell you quiet for the time being."

"Of course," Precious nodded.

"Justina's pregnant."

"Really!" Precious seemed stunned by the news. "So, you're going to be a father. I want to say congratulations but you don't seem excited."

"Maybe I would be if the child was mine but according to Justina the father is her new husband."

"Wait!" Precious put her hand up as if saying she needed a moment to process what Amir was telling her. "Justina is pregnant and married to another man?! When did all this happen? Weren't you all still a couple at Aaliyah's wedding?"

"When I came to the hospital, to see how Supreme was doing and get Justina, she broke up with me." Amir shook his head, still fuming over how callously he was dumped, by the woman he planned on marrying. "I thought Justina was at the hospital to console her best friend but she was really there keeping a vigil for Desmond Blackwell."

"The man who took the bullet for Supreme?"

"Yep."

"I'm assuming he's the man she also married."

"Yes. While she was in Miami, preparing to be a bridesmaid, she was fucking another nigga the entire time." Amir stood back up and began pacing again, as if trying to control of his anger.

"Amir, I know this is all fresh and your emotions are raw but in time it will get better. Justina's a beautiful girl but you might've dodged a bullet and should consider yourself lucky. Let's not forget who her mother is," Precious reminded him.

"We had moved past that. I thought Justina was my future."

"I'm not trying to be insensitive Amir but what does Justina breaking up with you have to do with you now feeling guilty about switching the paternity test?"

"What if the baby Justina's carrying is mine? The same way I tried to rob my dad of his relationship with his child, what if Justina is trying to rob me of mine?"

"Woah! That's a lot of speculating Amir, or maybe just wishful thinking on your part. Clearly you have deep feelings for Justina. Maybe you want the baby to be yours," Precious reasoned.

"Maybe. Right before I let you in, I was on the phone with Justina. She said the baby isn't mine. I can't lie, I was disappointed but I pray she was telling me the truth. Just the idea of her keeping my child from me, made me realize how cruel my actions were to my dad and Genevieve. I was trying to play God with their lives. No one has the right to do that, even if I was only trying to protect my mother."

"I'm glad you had a come to Jesus moment but it means absolutely nothing, if Genesis can't bring mother and daughter home safely. So, instead of whining about Justina and her pregnancy, save your prayers for Skylar and Genevieve because they're going to need them," Precious seethed.

Chapter Nine

Captive

Caleb was nodding off, ready to fall asleep when he heard shouting. "What the fuck!" he mumbled, raising his head up in the bed. His eyes darted towards his laptop. He wasn't sure if what sounded like a loud commotion, was coming from the hallway outside his hotel room door or from the surveillance he was doing.

The battery life on the GPS tracking device was about to die at any moment, so Caleb had started to get some much needed rest, believing he had no chance of obtaining information about

Skylar's and Genevieve's whereabouts. But when Caleb realized it was Arnez's voice he was hearing, a glimmer of hope was ignited.

Caleb jumped up out of bed and sat down in the chair at the desk his laptop was on, listening intently. *Please don't let the battery die!* Caleb was begging to himself as Arnez continued speaking to his worker. The yelling had now ceased and he was much calmer which allowed Caleb to hear what was being said more clearly.

"You're one hundred percent positive, Maverick's mother is missing?" Arnez questioned. "It's possible she simply went on vacation for a few days."

"Based on all the information I have, that's not the case. One of her neighbors says two police officers came to her house and she left with them. But when I checked the local precinct they had no record of anything regarding her. She hasn't been seen since."

"This isn't good," Arnez uttered. "I had a strong feeling before but now I'm positive Genesis has Maverick. I would've bet my life that Maverick would never give me up but if they have his mother, all bets are off."

"What you wanna do, boss?"

"I need to think for a moment."

"I think we need to leave here asap."

"I didn't ask you what you think!" Arnez snapped. "Besides anywhere we could go, Maverick would know to tell Genesis. And we just can't go anywhere with a baby but you're right, we can't stay here. I think I might know where we can go."

Skylar and Genevieve are there...Damn!" Caleb's heart was racing. *Arnez, just say where you're taking them next so I can find you,* Caleb said to himself.

"I need to make a stop. Get them together and be ready to leave when I return," Arnez said, grabbing the car keys.

"Of course, boss but are you sure we all shouldn't leave together now?"

"No, I have to make sure where we're taking them isn't problematic," Arnez informed his worker.

"So, you do have an idea where we gon' be staying?" the worker wanted to know.

"Yeah, I do. I'ma take them to..."

"Take them where? Go 'head and say it," Caleb mumbled, waiting in anticipation for Arnez to finish his sentence. "Fuck! Fuck! Fuck!" he barked, slamming his laptop close once he realized there was no longer any connection. The battery on the GPS had died, leaving Caleb with only one option.

$$$

Skylar was sitting on the couch watching an episode of SVU while holding Genevieve. She was beginning to fall asleep in her mother's arms. Skylar pressed pause on the remote so she could put her daughter down in the crib.

"My beautiful little baby girl," Skylar smiled, stroking her daughter's hair, taking in her scent before laying her down. She stood over Genevieve and within a few minutes, her eyes were closed, she had fallen into a deep sleep. Skylar was still in awe of her sweet baby girl like she was a newborn. She would've continued gazing at her but she was interrupted with the sound of the hidden door being unlocked. Skylar swallowed hard and she was overcome with that now familiar sinking feeling in the pit of her stomach. She dreaded every time the door opened, because Skylar knew it could be the day she was murdered and would never be able to hold her daughter again.

"Pack up you and your daughter's belongings...now!"

"Are we leaving...where are we going?" Skylar asked the man who she had seen numerous times but was never told his name. All she knew was he worked for Arnez.

"Someplace new, so get your stuff together."

"Genevieve just fell asleep."

"Well, wake her up," he ordered, glancing down at his phone. "I have to take this call. I'll be right back, so you better start packing."

Instead of packing, Skylar sat back down on the couch. She grabbed Genevieve's baby blanket and held it up to her chest. Since the day they were taken, Skylar wondered how long would it take for Arnez to learn the truth...Genesis wasn't the father of her daughter. The only reason she hadn't revealed the information was because Skylar knew she would be signing their death certificate. For the time being, Arnez thought of them as an asset to destroy his enemy. The day he thought of them as a liability, was the day they would die.

Skylar decided to let Genevieve sleep while she gathered up their belongings. Behind the hidden door, they basically had their very own one bedroom apartment. There was a living room, bathroom, washer, dryer and even a kitchen. Every few days, Arnez's worker would come and bring them groceries, hygiene and baby products or whatever else they needed. It wasn't on the penthouse level Skylar had been used to but the accommodations were comfortable. All of her and Genevieve's basic needs were met. Now they were being moved someplace else and Skylar wondered if this meant, soon they would be going home or if they were being sent to their permanent resting place. Once again, Skylar heard the door opening, shaking her out of her trance.

"Arnez just called and he'll be here in forty-five minutes. When he pulls up, we out the door immediately, so you need to..." before completing the sentence he stopped.

"Is there something..."

"Be quiet!" he barked at Skylar. "I think I hear something."

They both stood silent for a few minutes. Skylar could see him struggling to listen. Suddenly, he turned and walked off, leaving the hidden door open for the very first time. Skylar couldn't stop herself from running towards the entrance. For a brief moment, she felt free. Skylar stuck her head out, wanting to see what was on the other side of the door. There was a dark hallway and she wanted to see where it led to. Skylar glanced back at Genevieve to make sure she was still sleeping and then allowed her prying eyes lead her. She was almost at the end of the hall, when what sounded like an explosion erupted. Skylar damn near fell flat on her ass, racing back to what she hoped would be safety.

The noise was so loud, it caused Genevieve to awaken from her sleep. She was wailing and Skylar hurried to reach her. "It's okay, baby," she gently patted her daughter's back as she walked back towards the hidden door to close it.

"Move!" Arnez's man came bursting through the entrance waving his gun, almost knocking Skylar and Genevieve down. He then stepped back, firing off shots. An unseen gunman or men were returning fire. To Skylar's dismay, she and her daughter were smack in the middle of a gun battle and there was a chance, no one would make it out alive.

Chapter 10

One Option

What can best be described as the sound of a herd of bulls or a military stampede, echoed throughout the two-story home on the quiet dead-end street. More than a dozen men armed with Glock pistols, bulletproof vest, equipment belts with speed loaders for additional magazines and handheld transponder devices, stormed through each room in search of their targets.

"All clear, boss!" Zach, the leader of the small army who were trained to kill announced, pressing the 'push to talk' button on the handheld transceiver, clipped to his attire. Within seconds, Genesis stepped through the entrance, where the front door had been knocked down using a battering ram.

"No sign of Arnez?" Genesis questioned, upon entering the hallway of the house.

"There is a dead man in the room at the end of the hall. Not sure if it's Arnez," Zach said. "I also found a M84 stun grenade. It's non-lethal. It's designed to temporarily neutralize the enemy by disorienting their senses. I'm guessing that's how they were able to gain access to kill that man," he explained while Genesis was walking towards the back room.

"Nah, that ain't Arnez. I don't know who the fuck that is," Genesis said eyeing the dead body. "Maybe Maverick played me and this ain't even where Arnez has been hiding out," he continued.

"You might be right," Zach agreed. "What do you want us to do next?"

"Hold on…it looks like there might be another room behind this door. Did you check in here?" Genesis asked.

"No, I didn't. I had no idea there was another room," Zack said with confusion, following behind Genesis.

"It seems to be some sort of hidden room,"

Genesis said, understanding why Zach and the other men would've missed it.

"It's huge back here," Zach commented, before noticing the baby crib in the corner.

"Genevieve was here. This is hers," Genesis revealed, becoming choked up holding the blood soaked baby blanket. "Please don't let this be her blood," he sighed, seeing even more blood on the carpet. "Damn! We must've just missed them! This is fresh blood!" Genesis roared, picking up the baby crib and tossing it across the room.

"Boss, do you want me to look around and gather any of your daughter's belongings I see?" Zach asked, trying to say something that might calm Genesis down.

"Nothing in here belongs to Genevieve. Burn this muthafucka down," Genesis ordered, throwing the bloody baby blanket to the floor and storming out the room.

Genesis sat in the SUV and watched as the house his daughter and Skylar had been held captive, went up in flames. Knowing his daughter was within his reach but now she was gone and possibly dead, had him ready to go ballistic. Genesis stared at the blaze for a few more minutes before motioning his driver to go. He held his head down feeling like he was mourning for the third time. First, when he got the results saying Genevieve wasn't his daughter. Second, when Amir admitted he had the results changed and Genevieve was in fact his child but had been kidnapped by Arnez. And now, wrapping his mind around the fact, there was a very real chance his daughter was dead. Genesis became completely engrossed in his thoughts, he almost missed Lorenzo's call.

"Yeah." Genesis answered.

"I know this isn't a good time for you but we need to know. What do you want us to do with Maverick and his mother?" Lorenzo asked.

"Kill them," Genesis said without hesitation.

"Say no more, I'll make the call and get back to you once it's been handled."

"Sure thing," Genesis replied about to hang up but something stopped him. "Wait!" He shouted grasping his phone tightly.

"What's up?"

"Let his mother go."

"Are you sure?"

"Yeah. She doesn't know who we are and even if she did, I doubt she'd seek retribution. Plus, the aftermath of losing her son, is more heartbreak then any parent should endure," Genesis stated, reflecting on the pain he was harboring.

"I'll inform our men to move forward with killing Maverick but let his mother go," Lorenzo affirmed and hung up.

Genesis remained silent for the duration of the ride home. He was mourning his daughter on the inside without shedding any tears on the outside. But the walls of strength Genesis had built around himself, were beginning to crumble.

$$$

Arnez was turning the corner, when he abruptly pressed his foot down on the brake. At the end of the street, it was chock-full of police cars and firetrucks. "What the fuck is going on?!" Arnez shouted, circling around the street to get a better view of what was going on. He parked his car a short distance from the scene, got out and stood behind a rather large tree, not wanting to be seen.

His eyes filled with rage and suspicion. The home he'd spent the last few weeks hiding out at, had been burned to the ground. His mind shifted to the source of his rage...Skylar and Genevieve. They were his gateway to ruining Genesis for good and he didn't know if they had died in the fire, were taken or escaped. Arnez's mind then flipped to his worker. He wondered if he'd sold him out and left with Skylar and her baby. If so, that would explain why he wasn't answering his calls. Instead of going into panic mode, Arnez got back in his car and placed a phone call. When the man answered, Arnez wasted no time getting straight to the point.

"Dale, this is Arnez. I need your assistance... immediately."

Chapter Eleven

Life Altering

Talisa went into the master bathroom, tempted to step into the shower with Genesis. The steam blurred the glass but she could still see the water drenching his skin. She wanted to be close to her husband. Feel his body against hers but although he was within her reach, Genesis seemed so far away. Instead of going to her husband, Talisa went back into their bedroom and waited patiently for him to come out.

"I was about to go pour myself some wine, would you like a glass?" Talisa asked Genesis when he came out the bathroom and sat down on the edge of the bed. He was wearing the black & white stripes, wide leg silk pajamas, she got him a few weeks ago. She walked towards him, wanting to glide her hand across his bare chest.

"No, I'm good," he said adjusting the draw-string on his pajama pants.

"When you came home, you went right in the shower. You didn't tell me what happened earlier."

"I told you, I didn't find Genevieve."

"I know but did you get any other leads?"

"No."

"Baby, you seem so intense," Talisa said, placing her hand on his shoulder.

"I'm fine."

"What is wrong with you?" Talisa asked, feeling his body flinch at her touch.

"What do you think is wrong with me," Genesis stood up. "My daughter is missing and more than likely she's dead."

"Don't say that."

"You wanna act like you're so concerned."

"Of course I am!"

"Did you know Amir was gonna have the paternity results changed?"

"Genesis, how can you think I'm even capable

of something like that?"

"I didn't think my own son was capable of ripping my daughter away from me but he did. So, answer my question."

"No! I had no idea what Amir did," Talisa cried. "Our son made a mistake but it isn't his fault Genevieve was taken."

"A mistake," Genesis scoffed. "That's what you calling what Amir did…a mistake?! A mistake is when no real damage is done. So, this ain't no fuckin' mistake. It's life altering."

Talisa was prepared to try and defend her son but before she could, they heard the doorbell ring. "I'll get it," she said, hoping Genesis would call down.

"No, let me. I need to get out this room anyway." Genesis was on the verge of losing complete control. The dark cloud hovering over him, was spreading rapidly and showed no signs of slowing down. When he got to the door, Genesis opened it without even bothering to see who was there. His heart dropped.

"I think she wants her father," Caleb smiled, handing Genevieve over to Genesis.

Genesis was speechless as he held onto his baby girl. For a moment he even questioned was any of this real or was he experiencing some sort of dream sequence. But when he placed her face against his and Genevieve latched onto her father's finger, Genesis knew his daughter was home.

$$$

When Lorenzo and Nico stepped into the warehouse where Maverick was being kept, they walked into a bloodbath. Everyone was dead except the one person who they came to make sure had been killed.

"What in the fuck happened in here!" Lorenzo gasped.

"I think it's pretty obvious," Nico remarked, probing the dead bodies scattered throughout the building. "The question is, how in the fuck did this happen and where is Maverick?"

"Not here which ain't good. Now we have two known enemies walking around freely," Lorenzo shook his head. "Let me find out if Maverick's mother has already been let go," he said sending a text.

"Damn! Both them niggas missing and we still ain't got Genevieve and Skylar back. I'ma let you break the news to Genesis," Nico sighed.

"We don't have Maverick's mother either,"

Lorenzo told Nico, after getting a reply to his text message. "You think I should call Genesis, or go tell him in person? I know it's late but this is important."

"My man has been through enough today. Let him sleep," Nico suggested. "We'll put some extra men outside his building to make sure he don't get any unexpected visitors."

"Cool. I'll call the cleanup crew and go see Genesis first thing in the morning."

$$$

Precious woke up and her natural instinct was to lean over and reach for Supreme. When his side of the bed was empty, she remembered he was still out of town. She was tempted to go back to sleep but glanced at the clock and realized what time it was.

"Damn, I didn't mean to sleep this late," she mumbled, reaching for her phone. She saw a few missed calls, a good morning text from Supreme but it was the text from Aaliyah, that put the biggest smile on her face. Her and Dale had eloped and were now officially married. Precious was filled with joy knowing her daughter was finally happy. It felt like a heavy weight had been lifted off her soul. After replying to Supreme and Aaliyah, she noticed a text from Genesis. His message sent her heart racing. It was the incentive Precious needed, to get out of bed and get herself together asap.

Chapter Twelve

Over My Dead Body

Precious flew through the hall in search of Genesis. It didn't take long for her to find him. You didn't typically see a tall, extremely good looking man, wearing a designer suit and holding a baby, at the hospital. The first thing Precious did was hug Genevieve.

"Look at this sweet, beautiful baby girl," Precious gushed. Becoming excited, thinking soon Aaliyah would be a mother and she a grandmother. "I know you must be so relieved, your daughter is home."

"I am," Genesis said, staring at Genevieve adoringly. "You see I brought her to the hospital with me. I'm not letting her out my sight."

"I don't blame you. Any update on Skylar?"

"The doctor said her surgery went fine but she's still in a coma. They're still not sure if she's going to make it," he revealed to Precious.

"In your text message you didn't tell me what happened."

"It's a long story. Let's go sit down," Genesis said as Precious followed him, holding on to Genevieve's tiny hand.

"She looks healthy," Precious commented after they sat down.

"Yes, Thank God. I had a doctor examine her and he said she was in perfect condition."

"It's crazy but even after Skylar said the baby wasn't yours, it didn't sit right with me. I even cracked the other father must have some really good genes," Precious joked. "I mean look at her. She has your eyes. She's such a beauty."

"I wish I had listened to my gut instinct. When Skylar was in labor and I delivered our daughter, the moment I held Genevieve in my arms, there was no doubt in my mind, she was my child. But I allowed my rage to succumb to a lie. I hate myself for that."

"Genesis, you can't blame yourself. A DNA test was done and Skylar admitted she had been with another man. How were you to know the test had been tampered with."

"If I had listened to my heart, I would've known the test wasn't right. Because I didn't, I almost lost my daughter and Skylar might die. This little girl deserves to grow up with her mother and father," Genesis said, kissing Genevieve on her cheek.

"What happened to Skylar?"

"Caleb exchanged gunfire with a man working for Arnez. The man ended up shooting Skylar. Our daughter could've been shot too but Caleb said, Skylar used her body to shield Genevieve. She saved our daughter's life."

"That's what a mother does. They protect their child. Skylar loves Genevieve more than anything in this world and trust me, she has no regrets, taking the bullet to save her life."

"I know but she shouldn't have had to."

"I get what you're saying but let's back up for a second. Caleb...that name sounds so familiar. Isn't he a friend of Amir's?"

"Yep, that's him. He was at the party Talisa put together for Genevieve."

"That's what I thought. That young boy is

the one who found them and brought Genevieve home to you?" Precious was stunned.

"Yes but he's not a boy, he's a man. I always knew there was something special about Caleb and he continues to prove me right."

"Very impressive, indeed. How did it happen? I need more details," Precious insisted.

"Honestly, he showed up at my door so late last night and he was holding my daughter. Asking him a million questions wasn't a priority."

"Of course. That makes sense," Precious agreed.

"He assured me Genevieve hadn't been hurt but Skylar was shot and he brought her to the emergency room, before bringing our daughter home to me. I know how close you and Skylar are and you're also Genevieve's Godmother, so I thought you should know what was going on."

"Yes, thank you for letting me know. I've been so worried about both of them. I'm praying Skylar pulls through."

"Me too," Genesis said. Precious could see the grave expression on his face.

"Listen, I know you're thrilled to have your baby back but I also know you're an extremely busy man. If you ever need me to babysit, I would be more than happy to. I mean, I am her

Godmother."

"I appreciate the offer and I have a feeling, I'll be taking you up on it. Genevieve needs to be surrounded by as many loved ones as possible." While Genesis talked, Genevieve made little baby noises that made Precious smile.

"But I'll never let anything happen to her again. It'll be over my dead body," Genesis vowed.

$$$

"I came over as soon as I heard your message!" Amir exclaimed, giving his mother a hug. "Genevieve's home...where is she?"

"She's not here and neither is your father," Talisa said.

"Where are they?"

"The hospital. Skylar was shot. Genesis wanted to go to the hospital and check on her."

"Of course he did," Amir huffed.

"She is the mother of his child, Amir."

"I know and you're right. But I can see how it bothers you the way dad is so protective of Skylar."

Talisa wanted to deny what her son said but it would be a blatant lie. She didn't want to share Genesis's love with another woman. Talisa didn't want to sound selfish but she wanted to be the only one with a hold on her husband's heart.

"Amir, I know this is hard. It's difficult for me too but Skylar will always be a part of our lives. She's Genevieve's mother which makes her a member of our family too. We both have to accept it, or risk alienating your father."

"I've already done that. Sometimes I feel like he's done with me," Amir said, sounding defeated.

"He's disappointed but now that he has Genevieve back, the healing begins. Your relationship with your father will be back to normal before you know it," Talisa tried to reassure her son. "You can't..." Talisa paused when the doorbell rang. "We're not done talking about this. Let me answer the door but when I get back, we're going to finish this conversation."

That was the last thing Amir wanted to do. Being at odds with his father and it constantly being a topic of discussion was mentally draining for him. He wanted things to go back to the way they were.

"Amir, I'm glad you're here."

Amir turned around and saw Lorenzo walking into the den with his mother. "What's up, Lorenzo. I guess you heard the news."

"What news?" Lorenzo seemed confused.

"I didn't have a chance to tell him," Talisa said to Amir.

"Tell me what?"

"Genevieve is home," Amir stated.

"What! When did this happen?" Lorenzo was completely thrown off with the unexpected news.

"Late last night, that young man Caleb came over and he had Genevieve with him." Talisa was sharing this information with Lorenzo and Amir at the same time.

"Caleb!" Both men blurted simultaneously. Talisa nodded yes.

"You didn't mention Caleb was the one who brought Genevieve home," Amir said.

"Honestly, I didn't think it mattered. Caleb works for your father. I assumed he's been involved with trying to locate Skylar and Genevieve," Talisa explained.

"A few weeks ago, I did walk in on a meeting between my dad and Caleb. But I had no idea he was working so closely with him on this."

"Neither did I," Lorenzo admitted. "Regardless, it's a beautiful thing. Genesis has his daughter back. What about Skylar?"

"He's at the hospital with her now," Talisa

said. "Unfortunately, Skylar was shot."

"Oh wow! I hate to hear that." Lorenzo put his head down for a second. "With good news, the bad news always seems to follow. Talisa, would you mind if I speak with Amir alone for a moment?"

"No, I need to make some phone calls anyway. But Amir, don't leave without talking to me first," Talisa said before leaving the room.

"I didn't want to upset your mother or worry her," Lorenzo said, walking closer to Amir. "You already know Arnez is an issue for us but we had a close business associate of his, named Maverick in our custody. He's the one who gave us the location of where Skylar and Genevieve were being held. The plan was to kill him but when Nico and I went to where he was being held, he was gone and our men were dead. We're still trying to figure out how he escaped but Maverick has a lot of connections. It's not if he'll be seeking retribution, it's when. So you need to be careful."

"Does my father know?"

"Not yet. I came over to tell Genesis but of course he's not here. We do have extra security monitoring everyone coming in and out this building but you know how this game goes."

"I do know and I'll make sure to be on alert

at all times. But umm," Amir stroked the tip of his finger across his bottom lip for a second. He wanted to choose his words carefully. "What do you think about this Caleb thing? You don't find it a bit odd he was the one able to find Skylar and Genevieve all on his own?"

"I haven't spoken to your father, so I don't know all the details. Honestly, I don't think the how or why matters. Genesis has his daughter back and it's worth celebrating. Who cares if Caleb is the hero."

"You get no argument with me about that," Amir nodded.

"Well, I gotta go. Remember what I said... watch yourself," Lorenzo warned.

Chapter Thirteen

Choices And Consequences

"Nigga, I'm fuckin' happy you back!" Floyd jumped out his car and said being extra animated. He gave Caleb a hug.

"Yeah, I missed yo' simple ass too!" Caleb joked, as they walked into the club. "So this the spot you wanna have my birthday party at now?"

"Yep. The people at the other spot was catching an attitude cause I kept changing the date. I was like fuck 'em. We can take our paper elsewhere," Floyd laughed.

"This spot nice though. It seem a lil' more upscale," Caleb commented when they went inside. "You sure they ain't gonna mind us having it here?"

"You know money talk, nigga. You deserve some next level type celebration. It cost more but this shit official," Floyd grinned, feeling proud of himself for locking down the venue.

"It's the middle of the day and I like it. I know it must be lit at night," Caleb said, warming up to the idea of this birthday bash, Floyd begged him to have.

"I knew once you saw it, you be all in," Floyd grinned. "The manager probably in the back, cause I saw his car out front. I told him we were stopping by, so he should be out any minute. I can let him know it's a go."

"Yeah you do that. Shiffon just came in," Caleb said turning towards the door."

"What she doing here?" Floyd wanted to know.

"To get the rest of her money. She's headed out of town, so I told her to stop by here and get it before she left."

"Cool. I'ma talk to the manager, while you handle things wit' her."

"Shiffon, glad you could make it," Caleb smiled, greeting her at the entrance.

"Of course I was going to make it. I need my coins," she beamed.

"I know you all about yo' money and I got it right here for you," Caleb said, reaching into his olive, khaki, and black camouflage Givenchy Pandora backpack. "I know you headed out of town but do you have a minute to talk?"

"For you...definitely. It sounds serious," Shiffon commented taking the envelope of money Caleb handed to her.

"It is." Caleb led her to a booth and they sat down. "It's all there," he cracked, watching her count the thick stack of one hundred dollar bills.

"You can never be too careful. I learned that after being shafted a couple times when I first got into the game," Shiffon winked, continuing to count her money.

"I feel you but listen. Remember the dude Maverick, I had you swoop up?"

"Of course I remember Maverick," Shiffon said casually, remembering how she'd never been so attracted to a man who was her mark. She actually felt a little guilty, for kidnapping Maverick, knowing he would be killed but it was her job. "What about him?"

"I wanted you to watch yo' back because he escaped."

"What? I figured he was dead by now."

"He was supposed to be but somehow he got away. I thought you would want to know."

"Yes, thank you," Shiffon sighed, putting the money back in the envelope and into her purse. "I'm sure he wouldn't even recognize me. I had on one of my many wigs and done up with a ton of makeup. I'm good."

"I'm sure you are but it's always important to protect yo'self," Caleb stressed.

"I'm an assassin, it's comes with the territory," Shiffon flashed a smile.

"I know you be busy wit' yo' line of work but I'm having a birthday party here in a couple weeks and I'd like you to come."

"Your birthday party...really." Shiffon lightly tapped her stiletto shaped nails on the table top.

"You can come as my special guest."

"Caleb, are you asking me out on a date?" Shiffon frowned up her face, taken aback.

"Yeah, I am," he said confidently.

"How old are you?"

"Legal."

"Do you know how old I am?" she questioned.

"I don't care how old you are. I'm attracted

to you and I like you. Don't nothing else matter."

"It matters to me," Shiffon's eyes widened. "Honestly, if we just met in the streets, I would think you were older and probably go out on a date," she admitted.

"Then what's the problem?" Caleb placed his manicured hands down in front of Shiffon, revealing a Sky-Dweller Oyster 42mm Everose gold Rolex watch. "I'm attracted to you...you attracted to me."

"Caleb, ain't no denying you a very good looking young man. And yes, you act mature for your age but..."

"Here comes the but," Caleb shook his head and laughed. "Why there gotta be a but?"

"Because you're too young for me. I don't know exactly how old you are but from what I heard, you ain't even twenty-one yet. I prefer my men older, at the very least, you need to be around my age. You fall short of that by at least five years."

"Just come to my party. Not as my special guest or date but as a business associate. I mean we do work together on occasion," Caleb said charismatically.

"If I'm in town, then I'll come. Deal?"

"Deal. But we need to shake on it." Caleb

extended his arm. "That's the only way a deal is official."

"I guess it's official then," Shiffon giggled, grabbing Caleb's hand. *This nigga is fuckin' cute and tall, just the way I like them. Too bad he isn't a few years older,* she thought to herself. "Well, I better get going. Another job awaits me."

"A'ight," Caleb stood up to walk Shiffon to the door. "You be careful. Your line of work ain't the safest."

"Neither is yours," she shot back in a flirtatious tone before leaving.

"Muthafucka, you can close yo' mouth!" Floyd walked up from behind and cracked. "You was in the corner talkin' to Shiffon a long time. Let me find out you was over there talking nasty to that girl."

"We had business to discuss and I invited her to my party."

"Last week, you was shittin' on the idea of a birthday party, now you inviting folks, like you the one who put this together," Floyd clowned.

"Man, whatever," Caleb laughed. "But if this party will get me some time wit' Shiffon, I'm all for it."

"Hold on." Floyd stepped back and gave Caleb a peculiar look. "I was joking when I made my comment about Shiffon. I didn't think you was really interested in her."

"Why wouldn't I be? Was we not looking at the same woman who just walked out of here."

"I get it…she hella fine but she sets niggas up for a living and for the right price will kill them too." Floyd gave his best friend, the what the fuck are you thinking stare.

"I know what she does," Caleb shrugged with agitation.

"Nigga, duh! That's why I'm confused why you even entertaining the idea of dealing wit' Shiffon on that level. She runs with a crew of assassins and she's the head bitch in charge!" Floyd exclaimed.

"Listen, I ain't got to explain what I like to you."

"Nah, you don't cause I already know. You like her cause she seems like a challenge. Ever since we was kids, you only be interested in shit you ain't got no business fuckin' wit'," Floyd shook his heads. "Man, leave that woman alone," he flung his hand. "She dangerous. I don't care how fine Shiffon is, some pussy you got to steer clear of."

Caleb heard what Floyd said but he didn't really hear him though, because he chose not to. He made up his mind, Shiffon was the woman he wanted, even though he knew, she wasn't what he needed. But for Caleb, that was part of Shiffon's allure.

$$$

"How in the fuck did Maverick escape?!" Genesis shouted, slumping down in his office chair. "We had several men guarding him. They all end up dead but Maverick escapes. This nigga Houdini now!"

"Not Houdini but I'm guessing a very persuasive negotiator," Lorenzo announced to everyone in the room, when he got off the phone.

"What's that supposed to mean?" Nico questioned.

"Yeah, that's a vague statement. We need you to further explain," T-Roc added.

"Before you do, can you get from that corner and come closer. We shouldn't have to struggle to hear you," Nico scoffed.

"I see you still in a bad mood," Lorenzo remarked, leaning against the wall. "But I'll accommodate your request since what I'm about to say is important."

"Do tell." Genesis sat up straight in his chair, wanting some understanding as to how Maverick was able to slip away.

"Initially when Nico and I got to the warehouse and saw the dead bodies, everyone was accounted for but the next day when I was trying to figure all this shit out, I thought about something."

"Can you please get to the point!" Nico barked. Everyone eyed Nico with disapproval. They knew he had a lot on his mind, due to both of his daughters but they were all under stress and needed him to chill with the hostile attitude.

"As I was saying," Lorenzo continued, "I remembered that Raymond was supposed to be working the shift that night. But he wasn't one of the dead men."

"Are you sure, he was supposed to be working? We have a lot of henchmen on payroll," Genesis stated.

"I know and before I jumped to conclusions, I spoke to Miss Meka because she handled the scheduling for the different shifts. At first she said Raymond wasn't scheduled to work, so I let it go. But a few minutes ago, she sent me a text saying Raymond was scheduled to work but he switched shifts with Trent."

"Is Miss Meka positive? She could have the days mixed up," Genesis reasoned.

"I had my reservations too but I called Miss Meka after she sent the text. That's who I was on the phone with. When Trent's wife stopped by the office, to pick up the money we left for her, she made a comment to Miss Meka. She said, Trent would still be alive, if he hadn't filled in for Raymond. It was only then, Miss Meka remembered taking Raymond's name off the schedule and replacing it with Trent. So when I had her look in the book, it showed Raymond wasn't scheduled to work."

"So wait, you think Raymond got our men killed because he plotted with Maverick, so he could escape?" Nico asked.

"I do. Raymond has been working every single day since we brought Maverick in. When I had Miss Meka look at the books, on several of those days he was working double shifts. On the night Maverick escapes, it so happens to be the same night Raymond decides to let Trent cover his shift. I smell something foul," Lorenzo nodded.

"I hate to say it but I think Lorenzo right," Genesis agreed, fuming on the inside. "Raymond has been working with us for years. He betrayed our family, had our men killed...men who saved his life when they was out there battling in these streets. That foul muthafucka."

"If this shit is true, then we're in an even more vulnerable position. Raymond knows the ins and outs of how this organization is ran and I'm sure he's already shared it with Maverick," T-Roc said.

"Of course Raymond was privy to how we handle security but we're constantly switching up stash locations, so he doesn't have access to drugs or money," Genesis clarified. "But he's still a problem. We need to get our men on him asap. But not the security he normally works with. Bring in our other team."

"I'm on it," Lorenzo said, placing a phone call.

"I should've killed Maverick myself," Genesis seethed.

"You had no idea, one of our own would flip on us and align with the enemy," T-Roc stated.

"But I did," Genesis sighed.

"Come on, Genesis. You talkin' crazy," Nico shrugged. "Nobody could've known that."

"Maverick had this way about him. I've been in this game for a long time but even I had to admit, there was something about him I liked. The few times I spoke with him alone, I developed a certain level of respect. The only reason he turned on Arnez was to save his mother. And I don't even think it's because he liked Arnez, it's because he respects the game and the code of the streets. He was willing to die for it but not sacrifice his mother," Genesis explained.

"I see where you going with this but it doesn't exempt Raymond's foul ass," T-Roc scoffed.

"But I knew Maverick was a potential threat. If he can make a nigga like me, who lives and breathes this game, feel empathy towards him. Then I should've known, if given the opportunity, he could mind fuck a weak nigga like Raymond. The moment he gave me Arnez's location, I should've put a bullet in his skull."

"Then why didn't you?" Nico questioned.

Genesis laid his head back on the leather chair, staring up at the custom wood beamed ceiling. There was a long pause and he let out a deep breath before answering. "Because a part of me wanted to let him live. Now I have to deal with the consequences."

Chapter Fourteen

Dead Weight

Maverick opened the motorized window shades, allowing the natural light to brighten the opulent space. Overlooking the skyline and sparkling waters of the City Of Baltimore, the luxury condo on 200 International Dr. was a far cry from the warehouse he'd escaped less than a week ago. Yet Maverick still felt like a chained prisoner who was desperate to regain control of his life. He believed the only way to achieve this, was to eradicate everyone responsible for wreaking havoc on his life.

"What's on the agenda today?" Raymond entered the room, disrupting Maverick's thoughts.

"A couple dudes I deal wit' in BMore, are finally back in town. We're leaving here shortly to meet with them," Maverick said, glancing down at the gray hardwood floors. "Have you found out anything about the girl?"

"Not yet and I doubt I will. Like I told you, a dude named Caleb, who runs drugs for Genesis in Philly, is the one who brought her in. He used her before and guaranteed she could deliver the goods," Raymond said, taking a seat on the couch and turning on the television.

"At least try to find out what Caleb's last name is. If I locate him then I probably can find the girl," Maverick presumed.

"Maybe." Raymond shrugged his shoulders. "But I don't know Philly niggas like that, so the only way I could get the info, is placing calls to people in Genesis's inner circle or maybe Miss Meka but that'll raise too much suspicion," he said, as he continued to turn channels. "I'm supposed to be out of town, visiting family. How would it look, me calling asking about a nigga I ain't neva met."

'Who is Miss Meka?"

"She works for Genesis, Lorenzo and Nico.

Handling paperwork, scheduling, the warehouses, just a lot of different bullshit. I guess something like an office manager for drug operations," Raymond laughed.

"Then she must have access to a lot of information?"

"Yeah but like I said, with all the shit that went down, I'd look mad suspicious calling Miss Meka about this Caleb dude."

"There has to be another way," Maverick pressed, refusing to let it go.

"Man, fuck them niggas. I got you outta that warehouse. You free! I don't even see why we gotta go back to NYC. We can build shit up right here in Baltimore. Plus, this crib you got is sick." Raymond was damn near salivating at the thought of forever lounging in the over 6,000 sq ft. lavish accommodations.

"We better get ready to go. They waiting for us," Maverick said, grabbing the car keys.

Maverick remained consumed in his own thoughts as they headed to Silver Spring. He spent the first part of the ride, asking Raymond a million questions, specifically about the woman Miss Meka and how Genesis and his crew ran their drug operation. The second half of the ride, he barely heard anything Raymond was saying, just the sound of his voice. His rage was aimed in so many directions. Maverick had been in the game for years but this had been the closest he ever came to death. The moment he gave Genesis the location of where to find Arnez, he knew the clock was ticking. But there was no way he could watch his mother be tortured and killed. Maverick was built for the street life and if he died so be it but he didn't want his mother to suffer for his sins. In his heart, he believed Genesis was going to have his mother murdered regardless but he had to at least try and save her. So when Maverick escaped and found out her life had been spared, he realized Genesis wasn't the monster he thought. It eased his fury but didn't erase it.

Then there was Maverick's mixed emotions towards Shiffon. She enticed him and he felt like a weak nigga for falling prey to her seduction. Not only that, although he wanted her dead, he remembered how hard she made his dick and he still wanted to fuck her. That shit was driving him crazy.

"These niggas got a nice crib too. You and yo' people gettin' paper," Raymond commented when Maverick pulled up in the driveway. "I made the right choice switching to yo' team.

Pretty soon, I'll be living like this too," Raymond grinned getting out the car.

"Indeed. You came through. If it wasn't for you, I'd be dead right now."

"It was an easy decision. You kept yo' word and gave me a shit load of money and an opportunity to be a part of yo' team. I would've neva got that wit' Genesis and them. All they saw me as, was the help. What the fuck I look like doin' security for the rest of my fuckin' life," Raymond complained.

"I feel you," Maverick said, using a key to open the front door.

"This yo' crib too?" Raymond asked, when Maverick opened the door.

"Yeah but I let Cam and Micah live here since they run my business in the Maryland, DC area."

"Nice. You should let me oversee things down here. It ain't like I'm going back to New York."

"I can do that," Maverick nodded. "Set you up in a crib."

"Something nice like this or I can just live in that sick ass condo you got in Baltimore. Man, hoes would be throwing pussy at me if they thought that crib was mine," Raymond laughed.

"Nigga, it's so good to see you!" Cam and Micah shouted simultaneously, when Maverick and Raymond came into the house.

"It's good to see ya too." Maverick gave both men a hug. "With everything that happened with Trae, Eli and them niggas, I needed to see some fam."

"We feel you on that. Man, for a minute we didn't think we was ever gonna see you again," Micah confessed.

"Word to my mother, I been sick worrying about yo' ass," Cam laughed. "When you first called, I thought it was some prank call type shit. Man, when I realized it was really you, I felt like a kid at Christmas," he said hugging Maverick again. "Don't ever scare us like that."

"I'ma try not to. This here, is the man you both need to thank for saving my life," Maverick said, introducing Raymond.

"What up fellas," he said boastfully, shaking their hands.

"Let's sit down, so we can discuss our next move," Maverick said, as the men gathered in the den area. "We need to strategically plan how I want to handle this shit. First thing, is getting rid of all dead weight. With that being said, your services are no longer needed." With smooth swiftness, Maverick reached for the gun in the back of his pants and released two bullets in the side of Raymond's head. He was dead before his body hit the floor.

"Man, I thought you said I was supposed to kill him," Cam smacked.

"I didn't feel like waiting. I hate an un loyal mutherfucka." Maverick shook his head. "This nigga didn't think twice about taking out the crew he worked wit'. He sold them out for chump change and thought I was gonna let him be a member of my team. Fuck outta here! If he'll flip on them without hesitation, then you know he'll shit on me."

"Exactly!" Micah and Cam agreed.

"Fuck that nigga," Maverick spit, glancing over at Raymond's lifeless body. "We got business to discuss."

$$$

"She really is beautiful," Talisa smiled, watching Genesis feed Genevieve.

"I think so too," he said proudly. "Having her back, makes my life seem perfect again. Well, as perfect as someone's life like me can possibly be."

"Genesis, I hope you know I don't mind

helping you with Genevieve. Skylar's still in the hospital and no one is expecting you to take care of baby on your own."

"I have things handled. Skylar's mother is here, so she's able to help out when I have business to tend to."

"I know but I wanted you to also know that I'm here for you and Genevieve too."

"Thank you but like I said, I have this handled."

"Now that you have your daughter home, I'm hoping you can start making peace with Amir. He still feels so guilty for what happened."

"As he should," Genesis said, standing up, softly patting Genevieve on her back so she could burp.

"I completely understand you're going to be upset about what Amir did for a while but don't you think it's time to start mending your relationship with our son?"

"If and when I decide to work on my relationship with Amir, it will be my choice." Genesis made clear.

"If and when? Genesis, he is your son! Not some business associate or distant relative. Amir deserves his father," Talisa implored.

"So did Genevieve but that didn't stop Amir

from ripping her away from me. Now, I'm done with this conversation. My daughter needs me."

Talisa stared in disbelief as Genesis walked outside on the terrace, ignoring her pleas. He was kissing Genevieve on her cheek and then cradled her in his arms. Her husband seemed perfectly content to be submerged in a world that didn't include his wife. Talisa knew that had to change or their marriage wouldn't survive.

"Hi, I really need to see you and it can't wait. I'm on my way over," Talisa said, hanging up abruptly. She hadn't spent all those years away from her husband and child to just give up on her family. Talisa was prepared to fight and knew exactly who to align herself with.

Chapter Fifteen

Summer Games

"You coulda let a nigga know you was comin' through!" Caleb smiled, knocking fists with Amir.

"It was last minute. I had to handle some quick business in Virginia and thought I stop through Philly and see you," Amir said, handing his menu to the waitress. "Are you ordering something?"

"Nah, I'm good. I'd just finished eating when you hit me up. "But I'll take a Sprite, light on the ice," Caleb told the waitress. "So, how's everything wit' you...you good?"

"I'm straight but things could be better."

"Really? Profits have been up the last couple months. I assumed business was booming everywhere."

"Business is good, thankfully," Amir nodded. "I was speaking about my personal life. I'm sure you're aware of the rift between me and my father."

"I don't know the details," Caleb shrugged, reaching for the glass of Sprite the waitress placed on the table.

"I assumed with how close you and my dad had become, he would've mentioned it to you."

"I wouldn't call us exactly close," Caleb said fidgeting with his napkin.

"You are the one who brought Genevieve home. You can do no wrong in my father's eyes now...how did you find them anyway?" Amir inquired.

"I guess you can say I was lucky," Caleb nodded. "Man, that food lookin' good!" he commented, when the hot plate was placed in front of Amir. He was trying to move on from the topic of how he found Skylar and Genevieve but Amir wasn't having it.

"It was more than luck. I mean Nico, T-Roc, Supreme, Lorenzo...couldn't none of them find out where Arnez had taken them. You did good, no need to be modest," Amir smiled, sprinkling some pepper over his food.

"Not being modest. I did what anybody else would've done," Caleb said casually, glancing down at his phone. "This is my mother," he lied. "I'll be right back. I really need to take this call."

"Of course. Go 'head man, take your time."

Caleb knew the unknown number had to be Arnez calling him back. He'd missed his call earlier but got his voice message and wanted to make sure he answered this one. "Hello."

"Good thing you picked up. I would hate to think you turned on me."

"Arnez, calm down. That's yo' stress talkin'."

"What makes you think I'm stressed?"

"The urgent message you left on my phone. You sounded mad stressed to me."

"Things aren't working out as planned. I had to leave the location I was at," Arnez sighed.

"What happened?"

"I guess you can say, shit is blowing up in my face. Have you got the information I asked you about?"

"Amir has been pretty tight lipped about his dad. I think they might be on the outs right now, so I haven't gotten any information on this

Maverick dude."

"Dammit! I need to find him because this nigga in Miami tryna give me the run around," Arnez grumbled.

"You in Miami?" Caleb asked, wondering who Arnez knew there.

"Yeah but it doesn't look like I'll be here much longer, especially if I don't get this money."

"Man, I can send you some money," Caleb offered wanting to find out Arnez's exact location.

"The type of money I need, only Maverick can give me, that's why you have to find him. At this point, not even sure if he dead or alive but I need to know."

"Not sure what else I can do. I don't have any dealings wit' Genesis, only Amir and he ain't telling me shit."

"There might be another way."

"Tell me what it is and I'll do it," Caleb stated.

"There's a dude named Micah who works closely with Maverick. If anybody would know if that nigga dead or not, it would be him."

"Why don't you call him?"

"The last number I had on him, ain't working. Which isn't surprising because he do switch it up a lot for security purposes. But I do have an address, that I know is still good."

"Okay, so do you plan on going there when you leave Miami?" Caleb questioned.

"I can't wait that long. I need you to go."

"Go where?"

"Maryland."

"Arnez, I don't feel comfortable rollin' up on that man's crib in Maryland. He don't know me. I knock on his door, he apt to put a bullet in my chest."

"Don't worry, I got you covered. I'ma text you the address and also a code word to give Micah when you see him. He'll know you legit."

"Cool."

"Leave first thing in the morning. The earlier the better. I'll be back in touch tomorrow."

Dealing with Arnez was taking a toll on Caleb. He wanted to be done with him but Arnez kept pulling him in. Now he was adding a new enemy of Genesis's in the mix. Caleb didn't need to drive down to Maryland, he already knew Maverick was very much alive and he had no interest in linking up with him or one of his workers. But what choice did Caleb have. He could keep playing Arnez's game, until given the right opportunity to kill him or finally come clean to Genesis but risk losing his job and life. Killing

Arnez, seemed like the better option and Caleb remained committed to it.

$$$

"That was fast." Precious said, when she opened the door to let Talisa in.

"Said I was on my way." Talisa hurried in, tossing her purse and keys on top of the 3-tiered curved console table in the entry hallway.

"You did, I just didn't realize you meant literally. Can I get you a drink...something strong, like maybe a shot?" Precious suggested. "You appear a bit rattled which is so not you," she said, walking over to the bar and pouring Talisa a shot of tequila.

"Thanks." Talisa grabbed the shot glass and quickly swallowed, in one take. "My marriage is in trouble," she gasped, handing Precious her glass for a refill.

"How about we hold off on another drink until we figure out what's troubling you." Precious sat down on the chair across from Talisa. "I'm a little surprised you decided to speak with me about your marital concerns. We're not exactly close."

"True but you are close to all parties involved,

plus from what I heard, you're a skilled schemer. No offense."

"No offense taken." Precious crossed her legs, adjusting her navy satin, polka dot twist front shift dress. "Before discussing a scheme, what seems to be the problem?"

"Genevieve."

"Amir already tried getting rid of Genevieve and I was very disappointed at the lengths he went to, in order to make it happen. Please don't tell me you were a part of that because if you were..."

"No!" Talisa interjected. "I would never try and keep Genesis away from his child. What Amir did was wrong and I want to make things right but Genesis is shutting me off. I think he believes I'm responsible."

"Like you had something to do with what Amir did?"

"Yes. He even asked me if I played a role. I was stunned and hurt, he could even think such a thing. But Genesis feels so betrayed by our son, he isn't being rational."

"Can you blame him? He almost loss his daughter for good and Skylar may never recover."

"I understand and Amir is dealing with the aftermath but I'm not the enemy. I'm not trying to replace Skylar but I'm Genesis's wife. He needs to allow me to have a relationship with Genevieve. The closer he becomes to her, the more he pushes me away. We haven't even had sex since she's come home. I mean we used to have sex..."

"Hold that thought," Precious put her finger up. "Let me pour myself a drink first." Precious was far from a prude but she had no clue, discussing Talisa's sex life with Genesis, was on the agenda.

"It's like he doesn't trust me to be alone with his daughter. Like he must protect Genevieve from everyone, including me," Talisa complained.

"Then we just have to make Genesis see you can be trusted with his daughter."

"He's making it impossible. I volunteered to stay with her while he works but he said Skylar's mother is here and she can watch Genevieve. And remember that day, he had you babysit."

"Well, I am her Godmother," Precious stated proudly.

"I know but I was home. There was no reason for him to get Genevieve dressed, gather her toys and other belongings to bring her here."

"I'll admit, I did assume you were either away or unavailable. I even suggested I come over to your place and watch her but Genesis declined."

"You see I'm not being paranoid about this," Talisa shook her head becoming distraught. "He's chosen his daughter and is pushing me away, when there's room for both of us."

"You're absolutely right, there is and Genesis needs to be reminded of that. Tomorrow, your husband will be needed at his office and I'll make sure myself nor Skylar's mother is available. Which will leave only you, so be ready for baby duty."

"You're not wasting any time. I like that!" It was the first glimpse of optimism Talisa revealed since arriving at Precious's door.

"I've had plenty of experience with relationships, plus I've been married, divorced, an annulment and remarried. Through my colorful dealings with men, one thing I've learned, is you don't want your husband to feel disillusioned. That quickly leads to hopelessness which is very painful and toxic for a marriage. From everything you said to me, Genesis has crossed that line and we need to act quickly."

"I agree. I'm so glad I came to you." Talisa stood up and hugged Precious tightly. "I see why my husband thinks so highly of you. You're a closer."

"I'm glad I was able to put some enthusiasm

in your voice. Now, go home and get plenty of rest. You have a very busy day tomorrow and I have phone calls to make. We'll chat tomorrow," Precious said walking Talisa to the door.

Once Talisa was gone, Precious walked over to the fireplace and stared at a picture of Skylar holding Genevieve. She wasn't helping Talisa just to save her marriage but also for Skylar, who she considered to be a very close friend. Precious knew there was a real chance, Skylar would never wake up from her coma. If that happened, Genevieve needed a mother. Someone to love her, like she was their very own. In her heart, Precious believed Talisa could be that person. She wanted to do everything in her power to give her Goddaughter the life she deserved and the one Skylar would also want for her.

Chapter Sixteen

Deadly Dilemma

Arnez lurked from a distance, eyeing the waterfront estate located along the Biscayne Bay in the trendy Upper East Side of Miami. Once the timing was right, he bypassed the lush gardens with mature trees and headed up the circular driveway. *I've finally arrived,* he thought to himself before pressing his finger on the doorbell. It took a few minutes for someone to come to the door but with such a large home, Arnez figured as much.

"What are you doing here? My wife could've been home!" Dale barked when Arnez showed up at his front door.

"I waited to make sure your lovely, pregnant wife, was long gone, before ringing the doorbell," Arnez smiled. "You left me no choice but to come over after ignoring my calls."

"We just got back in town from an extended honeymoon. I told you I would be in touch, once I got settled in," Dale said, blocking Arnez from entering his home.

"I don't have the luxury of waiting for you and your new wife to get settled in." Arnez and Dale were standing eye to eye. Dale wasn't budging but neither was Arnez. "I'm not leaving until we talk. Do you want Aaliyah to come home and see me here? I don't think that sort of stress, would be good for the baby."

"Don't say Aaliyah's name or mention my unborn child again. Are we clear?"

"We're clear."

"Good. You have five minutes." Dale stepped to the side and let Arnez inside.

"Since I'm working on very limited time, I'll get right to the point. Your brother and I had a very lucrative business arrangement going but prior to his death, Emory owed me a substantial amount of money. Before, I was in a financial position to let it go but things have changed.

I think it's only right, you make good on your brother's debt and I'm here to collect."

"Whatever arrangement you had wit' my brother, had nothing to do wit' me. Matter fact, if Emory had never gotten involved wit' you and Maya, he would still be alive. So I don't owe you shit!" Dale spit.

'"You placing your hostility towards the wrong person. It's your father-in-law who pulled the trigger and killed your brother. How does it feel looking into Aaliyah's face, knowing her daddy is the one who put a bullet in Emory's head," Arnez mocked.

"You sonofabitch!" Dale lunged at Arnez, knocking him down on the marble floor. He jumped on top of him with his fist balled up. Dale landed his first punch on Arnez's chin, causing his neck to twist to the side. He swung on him one more time, busting his lip. "You get the fuck out my house and don't ever come here again," Dale threatened, clutching Arnez by the throat. "If you do...you a dead man!" He released him from his grip, slamming his head down on the floor before getting up.

"You should've gave me the fuckin' money." Arnez stood, spitting the blood out his mouth. "Now you the dead man."

Dale was ready to whoop on Arnez again but became distracted when he heard the front door open. With the intention of only allowing Arnez to stay for a few minutes, Dale made the mistake of leaving the door unlocked. When he saw the Haitian killers storm in, armed with machetes and guns, Dale knew Arnez was correct...he was a dead man.

Dale closed his eyes, ready to die. P*lease protect over Aaliyah and our child,* were his final thoughts as the machete ripped through his neck, almost severing his head.

$$$

"Man, I appreciate you making this ride wit' me," Caleb turned and said to Floyd as they drove down I-95 S, towards Maryland.

"Nigga, you know I wasn't 'bout to let you go down here by yo'self. I can't let nothin' happen to you, we got a birthday party coming up!" Floyd cracked, rolling up his window.

"You actin' like we celebrating yo' birthday."

"We best friends...we share everything," Floyd grinned. "The party gon' be so lit. You know how many muthafuckas hittin' me up for an invite. Niggas and chicks I ain't heard from in a minute. Speakin' of chicks, what's up wit' you and Shiffon? Is she coming to the party?"

"Ain't nothin' up wit' us and I doubt she coming. I haven't heard from Shiffon since she stopped by the club for her final payment. I guess it's clear, she only interested in a business relationship," Caleb shrugged.

"Good. She ain't for you no way."

"Why you say that?"

"For one, she a killa. That should be enough but for yo' crazy ass, I know that ain't a deal breaker." Floyd gave Caleb a side eye.

"A'ight muthafucka, you can move on to yo' next reason."

"She too old. Hell, I don't even know how old Shiffon is, so I ain't even just talkin' age but you can tell she a seasoned broad. You don't need nobody like that in yo' position."

"What tha fuck that mean...my position?"

"Nigga, you practically runnin' the drug game in Philly. And the OG himself, Genesis seem to fuck wit' you the long way. At this rate, you in line to be the king. Shiffon too street savvy to be yo' queen. You need somebody like Mia. She's already proven to be loyal."

"Mia ain't my type," Caleb said, brushing off Floyd's assessment.

"Why...because she's too normal for yo' taste?"

"Man, it sound like you like Mia. Why don't you date her?!"

"Nah, Kecia the only girl for me."

"You been wit' Kecia since the 6th grade."

"Damn right and I'ma stay wit' her too, cause she loyal! You need a girl like that too. Trust me. You remember my Uncle Tommy and what happened to him, dealing wit' snake ass Bridget."

"Bridget was a thief, who stole from yo' uncle and ended up gettin' him killed."

"Exactly! He knew she had a reputation for robbing niggas but he thought he could change her and it cost him his life. I don't want that to happen to you."

"Shiffon is nothin' like Bridgette but it don't even matter. Like I said, she only interested in a business relationship and nothin' else," Caleb huffed, as he slowed down, noticing his exit was about to come up.

"Caleb, I'm not tryna upset you. I'm only keepin' it real. You like my brotha."

"No, you are my brotha," Caleb turned to Floyd and said. "It's all good. But enough about Shiffon. According to this GPS, we'll be to Micah's place in less than five minutes. Let's focus on that shit."

"Like you always say, business first."

"And don't ever forget it," Caleb said, fist pounding Floyd as he turned down Warrenton Cv. He slowed down, eyeing the spacious homes that were spread far apart, on the tree lined street. "There it is." Caleb pointed to the house at the end of the cove.

"You want me to go to the door wit' you?" Floyd asked when Caleb pulled into the driveway.

"Nah, you stay in the car. If anything seems funny, then you know what to do," Caleb said, reaching in the back of the truck, retrieving two assault-style rifles.

"I'm ready for whatever." Floyd got in position, prepared to pull the trigger.

Caleb headed towards the door, hoping there would be no need for Floyd to use the weapons but in situations like this, you never know. But it was worth the risk for Caleb, if it meant luring Arnez back to Philly and making sure he was a dead man. First, he rang the doorbell. After a few minutes of no one coming to the door, Caleb started knocking.

"Damn! This nigga ain't home," Caleb huffed, turning to head back to his truck. Before he reached the halfway point, he saw two cars coming down the street and then accelerating on the gas towards him.

"Get tha fuck down!" Cam jumped out the first car so fast with his Glock aimed at Caleb, he barely had a moment to think. But when Floyd leaped out the truck with the assault rifles in both hands, Caleb knew he needed to speak up before a bloodbath erupted.

"Fuck! What's the code word," Caleb mumbled, knowing this was the wrong time to forget some shit. By now, Micah was on the scene with his gun drawn too. Floyd was debating whether he should just start shooting or wait to see what Caleb wanted him to do.

"What we doing!" Floyd shouted, keeping his eyes on both men. He was afraid if he looked away for one second, he would blow any chance of him and Caleb coming out of this alive.

"You ain't doin' shit but puttin' down those muthafuckin' guns, unless you ready to die!" Cam barked.

"Nah nigga! Not I. We either both laying down guns or we both dying!" Floyd spit back, jabbing his weapons forward.

"You don't wanna do this! It's two of us and you the only one strapped. When we fire, we ain't missing," Micah warned Floyd, who was standing tall although he was barely 5'6.

"Fulton Street!" Caleb shouted. "Fulton Street!" he shouted again, to guarantee he was heard, with all the commotion going on.

Micah and Cam both took their eyes off Floyd for the first time and set their attention on Caleb. "What the fuck did you say?" Micah questioned.

"Fulton Street!" Caleb shouted. His breathing had become rapid due to the overwhelming pressure he was under. "It's the code word Arnez gave me. He said not to mention his name, until I gave you the code word because it's the only thing that would matter."

"He told you right," Micah said, glancing over at Cam. Both men eased up and seemed to relax but Floyd was still maintaining his stance. He needed more convincing the threat was over.

"Arnez sent me here to see a dude named Micah. This is where he's supposed to live. Is that one of you?" Caleb was praying the answer was yes. He couldn't deal with having to meet anyone else today.

"Yeah, I'm Micah," he acknowledged, putting his gun down. "Why didn't you speak up from jump with the code word. We wouldn't of gone so gully on ya," he chuckled.

"Real talk, I froze," Caleb hated to admit. "The both of you came driving up so fuckin' fast, I didn't have time to think. Man, I felt like I was in a scene from Menace To Society," Caleb joked but was dead ass.

Both Micah and Cam laughed. "I feel you." Micah reached out his hand and shook Caleb's hand. "And your name?"

"Caleb and that's Floyd."

"As I told you, I'm Micah and that's Cam." As Cam was walking up, Micah glanced over at Floyd. "You can tell yo' man it's okay for him to lay down the guns."

"Floyd, we good," Caleb assured him.

"Come on in," Micah nodded, taking out his house keys.

"Floyd, I'm sorry man," Caleb told his best friend as they trailed behind Micah and Cam.

"No need to apologize."

"'Nah, my fuck up could've cost us both our lives."

"But it didn't. Shiiit, if I was gonna die wit' anyone, I would want it to be you."

"You my nigga for life." Caleb nudged Floyd on his shoulder.

"Can I get ya' anything?" Micah offered, once

they were all inside the house." Both Caleb and Floyd declined.

"So how long you been working for Arnez?" Cam questioned when they sat down.

Not that long...maybe like a year or so," Caleb answered.

"He must trust you a lot to send you here with the code word," Micah said, replying to a text.

"I've proven myself to be a loyal worker, so yeah he trust me."

"What does Arnez need from me?"

"He's been trying to get in touch wit' a dude named Maverick." Caleb caught Micah and Cam briefly exchanging glares but he pretended not to. "He has concerns he might be dead."

"Do you have a number for Arnez?"

"No. He's laying low right now. I have to wait for his call. Arnez said he tried reaching out to you but the number was no longer good," Caleb explained.

"True. I tell you what. Take down my number and give it to Arnez next time he calls," Micah said, giving Caleb his digits.

"Okay but I'm sure his first question will be if Maverick is dead or alive. What should I tell him?" Caleb asked.

"Tell him to call me." Micah remained tight lipped.

"Cool. I'm sure I'll be hearing from Arnez soon and I'll give him the message. Thanks for yo' time." Caleb shook both men's hands and left out with Floyd.

"It started off crazy but we leaving wit' what we came for," Floyd commented when they were back in the truck.

"Yeah, but I can't help but wonder why the nigga didn't want me to know Maverick is alive," Caleb said backing out the driveway.

"Cause maybe the nigga dead and they tryna keep that shit under wraps," Floyd reasoned.

"Nah, that nigga is very much alive."

Floyd turned in his seat and frowned up his face. "How tha fuck do you know that?"

"I just do." Caleb hadn't made Floyd privy to everything that went down. Mainly his role with having Maverick kidnapped. When he brought in Shiffon for the job, Genesis made it clear, he didn't want anyone to know Arnez had taken his daughter or what he was prepared to do to get her back.

"What you a psychic now?" Floyd mocked.

"Just a feeling. But like you said, we got what we came for," Caleb stated, turning up the radio.

If Micah does his part, this will all be over soon, Caleb thought to himself. *I just need Arnez's snake ass back in Philly, so I can kill him and he'll be outta my life for good.*

Chapter Seventeen

One Accord

"Baby, what's wrong?" Talisa asked, after watching her husband place several phone calls and sending numerous text messages.

"Nothing. I'm fine!" Genesis exclaimed, as he went into Genevieve's bedroom and started packing her baby bag. When he took his daughter out of her crib and started to dress her, Talisa felt this was the perfect time to make her move.

Where are you taking Genevieve? There's a heat advisory. Do you really think it's safe for her to be out?"

"She'll be fine. My driver will already have the AC on when we get in the car," Genesis said, as he continued to dress her.

"Are you taking her to see Skylar at the hospital?"

"No."

"Then where?"

"There's an emergency at the office and I have to go handle it. But I can't reach Skylar's mother, the nanny or Precious, so I'm taking Genevieve with me," Genesis begrudgingly explained.

"Genesis, let her stay here with me."

"It's better if Genevieve comes with me."

"No," Talisa said, gently placing her hand on top of Genevieve's hand. "It's better if she stays home with your wife, so you can focus on work."

Genesis stared deeply into Talisa's eyes searching for a clue, or an answer if leaving his daughter with her, was the right thing to do. Talisa could see him struggling, so she pushed harder to make her case.

"I love Genevieve but if you don't trust me to be alone with her, then why don't I come with you," Talisa suggested. "That way, I can stay with her, while you handle business. She doesn't need to be around any chaos and you don't need to be distracted. If you don't think I'm capable of taking care of her here, then going with you, sounds like the only solution."

Genesis looked down at his daughter, then back up at his wife. "I know you're capable," he slightly stuttered.

"Then what's the problem?" she questioned innocently.

"There is no problem. You're right, it probably is better if Genevieve stays home," Genesis reluctantly conceded. "You know she likes to be..."

"Genesis," Talisa stopped her husband before he could finish his sentence. "I know what Genevieve likes and I know her feeding schedule. I've been watching you take care of her for the last few weeks. We'll be fine. Don't worry about us. Go handle your business."

"Hopefully, I won't be gone long but call me if she needs anything," Genesis said, kissing Genevieve before leaving out.

"It's just us two," Talisa smiled picking Genevieve up. "You really are a beautiful baby girl and I do adore you. Now, I only have to convince your daddy." Talisa was determined to do just that.

$$$

"Nico, I wasn't expecting to see you here," Lorenzo said, getting out his car.

"I got a text from Miss Meka," Nico told him, closing his car door.

"I guess Supreme and T-Roc did too." Lorenzo nodded towards the Aston Martin and Lamborghini pulling up.

"I see Supreme still likes to accumulate toys," Nico remarked when he parked his Lambo next to Lorenzo's Range Rover.

"So what is this group meeting about?" T-Roc asked, as the men headed inside the warehouse.

"In the text, Miss Meka said Genesis set it up but he the only one that ain't here," Lorenzo said, unlocking the door.

"You know Genesis is always the last one to arrive, plus he on daddy duty now," Nico cracked. "I'm sure he'll be pulling up any minute," flipping on the light switch.

"I have a feeling this meeting wasn't Genesis's idea," Supreme sighed, being the first one to see the dead body chained to the chair.

"Is that a tongue on his lap?" T-Roc balked. "I didn't know muthafuckas was still doing that shit.

"Yeah, cutting tongues out ain't gon' neva

stop. Raymond learned the hard way, aligning himself with Maverick was the wrong move," Lorenzo shook his head. "That nigga did talk too much."

"He sure did. How else would Maverick know about Miss Meka," Nico fumed. "You know this means Miss Meka's probably dead. She isn't answering her cell or the office number."

"That nigga has quite a sense of humor," Supreme grimaced. "Leaving Raymond's dead body at the same warehouse we had him stashed, in the same chair and chains. Maverick sent us a message and we definitely received it," he said, putting his head down.

"Genesis isn't answering his phone neither. Do you think he's okay?" T-Roc dialed his number again, becoming more concerned.

"I'm sure Genesis got the same text as us. For whatever reason, he isn't here yet but I don't think anything happened to him. This ain't about Maverick taking us out, he's fuckin' wit' us," Supreme said, making eye contact with each of them. "The real question is, what's our next move?"

"Murder."

"Genesis!" All them turned and said in unison when they heard his voice.

"Man, you can't sneak up on us like that.

Not wit' this nigga's dead body behind us," T-Roc huffed.

"I just got back from the office. The place was in complete disarray. And I think Miss Meka's dead," Genesis said somberly.

"I knew it!" Nico shouted. "Maverick did this nigga a favor!" he raged. Kicking over the chair Raymond was chained to, knocking his dead body to the cement floor. "Miss Meka was a mother and a grandmother. She didn't deserve to die."

"You're right." Genesis sounded like he was carrying the weight of the world on his shoulders. "This is all on me. I should've killed Maverick when I had the chance. I'm slipping."

"Fuck all that!" T-Roc stepped forward. "If you slippin', then we all slippin'," T-Roc barked, moving his arm around the group of men, in a circular motion. "Cause we in this together. We done been through too much bullshit, to let this nigga Maverick have you questioning if you built for this. Hell, we is this! The five of us, we moving as one."

"T-Roc is right," Supreme agreed. "We got this."

Genesis, Supreme, Lorenzo, Nico and T-Roc stood together in one accord. They understood there was strength in numbers and planned to use it to their advantage.

$$$

When Genesis finally returned home, the only thing he wanted to do was hold his daughter in his arms. She represented everything he felt he was lacking and more. Genevieve was pure and innocent. The cruel world hadn't yet shattered her soul and Genesis wanted to protect her from that, for as long as possible.

"You're home," Talisa smiled when Genesis came into Genevieve's bedroom. Talisa was sitting on a chair, rocking her to sleep.

"Yes. I'm sorry for getting back so late."

"You don't have to apologize. Genevieve and I had a fun filled day. She's exhausted but I think she's trying to wait up, so her daddy can put her to sleep," Talisa said, placing Genevieve in her husbands' arms.

"I missed you something terrible," Genesis beamed, kissing his daughter on her forehead. Her heavy eyes were barely able to stay open. After a few more minutes of him cradling Genevieve, she fell asleep.

"Thank you for taking care of her while I was gone," Genesis said, putting Genevieve in her crib, with her new favorite blanket.

"You don't have to thank me. It was my pleasure. Hopefully, you'll allow me to stay with her again."

"I think that's a great idea," Genesis said turning on the baby monitor before closing Genevieve's bedroom door. "You were also right."

"Right about what?"

"Having Genevieve stay with you while I handled business. I didn't think my day was ever gonna end. All I wanted to do, was get home to my daughter and my beautiful wife." Genesis wrapped his arms around Talisa's waist and pulled her close.

"Sounds like you had a stressful day. What happened?"

"A lot...too much. But I don't wanna talk about work right now. I wanna savor being here with you. Coming home, seeing you holding my daughter so peacefully, made me realize how blessed I am to have you."

"I feel blessed to have you too."

"I know lately, I haven't shown how much I love and appreciate you. For that I'm sorry. You and Genevieve mean the world to me."

"Stop apologizing. My love for you is unconditional and I feel the same way about Genevieve. It's important to me that you know that. Just because I didn't give birth to her, doesn't mean I don't love her, Genesis, because I do."

"I see that clearly now and it makes me love you even more," Genesis declared, leaning down to kiss Talisa on her lips as he began to undress her.

Talisa welcomed her husband's embrace and the scent of his body against hers. She had been craving his touch for so long and their lovemaking was way overdue. For the first time in weeks, she felt connected to Genesis. He was no longer pushing her away, instead he was sliding every inch of his rock hard dick inside her wetness. The lips between her legs welcomed each powerful thrust. His tongue played with Talisa's nipples, as he enjoyed seeing her desire of wanting more, etched across her face. Genesis continued pleasuring every part of Talisa's body, while she begged for more and he was more than willing to give it.

Genesis and Talisa continued to make love all night. In their bed, on the terrace, in the shower, until ending back in bed again, holding one another closely. The hazy shade, that had been sucking the life out of their marriage, parted ways and the light of love was now able to shine down on them. Talisa rejoiced, knowing her husband was back home, not only physically but most importantly, mentally too.

"You know I love you more than anything in this world," Talisa softly whispered.

"Yes, and my love runs just as deep or even more," Genesis professed, before the soulmates fell asleep wrapped in each other's arms.

Chapter Eighteen

Fork In The Road

Precious's mind was lost in the clouds, as the nose of the private jet gently lowered to commence descent into Miami. She'd been replaying the phone call she received in the early morning hours, regarding her beloved daughter Aaliyah. It still didn't seem believable to her but it was all too real. Precious had been trying to reach her daughter for days without any luck and then the call came.

Once the plane landed, Precious had the driver take her straight from the airport to the hospital. She wanted to see Aaliyah's face and be there when she woke up.

"Hi, I'm Precious Mills. I'm here to see my daughter, Aaliyah Clayborn," she told the lady at the front desk.

"Yes, Mrs. Mills, her doctor is expecting you. Hold on for one moment, so I can page him. He wanted to speak with you, before you went to see your daughter," the lady explained.

Precious didn't have all the facts of what happened to her daughter but she knew none of it was good. Her fears were growing and she was consumed with dread.

"Mrs. Mills," the doctor called out before touching her shoulder from behind. "I'm so sorry. I didn't mean to scare you," he said, when her body flinched at his touch. "I was saying your name but you didn't respond so..."

"No! Please don't apologize," Precious said cutting him off. "I can barely hear my own thoughts right now."

"I understand. I'm Doctor Blanton and I've been treating your daughter. Can we sit down for a moment?"

"Yes, of course. I have so many questions. I still can't believe my daughter has been here for almost a week and I was just notified. I even called her husband to find out what was going on but I haven't been able to reach him," Precious said, trying her best to keep her cool.

Doctor Blanton glanced down at some notes on his clipboard and then back up at Precious. "Her husband, is that Dale Clayborn?"

"Yes! Is he in the hospital too?"

"Unfortunately Mr. Clayborn is deceased."

"Dale is dead?!" Precious's eyes widened in disbelief, putting her hand over her mouth, hesitant to ask her next question. "Is my..."

"No, your daughter isn't dead," the doctor quickly assured her.

"Thank you God." Precious lifted her head and hands up and said.

"But I'm sorry to inform you, the baby she was carrying didn't make it."

Tears rolled down Precious's cheeks. She was looking forward to being a grandmother for the very first time. And watching Aaliyah embark on motherhood. Those dreams were now shattered.

"Does Aaliyah know?"

"Not yet. I don't have all the details, so I advise you to speak with the Miami Dade police. From what I understand, your daughter and her husband were found by the maid. They had been there for a couple days. She wasn't physically hurt but extremely dehydrated."

"Is that the reason she lost the baby?"

"The delay in getting her medical attention didn't help but there were other complications with your daughter's pregnancy."

"I see," Precious pined. "I did speak with the police. They said, Aaliyah placed a 911 call but the call was routed through the nearest cellphone tower to a neighboring county's 911 system, and the dispatcher couldn't locate the address from where the call was coming from. Something crazy," she shook her head. "No one mentioned Dale's death to me over the phone, although they did tell me to come by the police department after I left the hospital because they had some questions for me."

"I know this must be a difficult time for you and if I can help in any way, please don't hesitate to ask."

"Thank you. Can I go see Aaliyah?"

"Your daughter is stable but she's heavily medicated. She's been sleeping most of the time but Aaliyah seems to be very traumatized."

"Isn't that normal for everything she's been through?"

"Yes. It's to be expected for her to experience

some trauma. But once she's cleared to leave the hospital, keep a close watch over your daughter, at least for the first couple weeks," Doctor Blanton advised.

"Is there something you're not telling me, doctor?"

"No, I don't won't you to worry. Physically, your daughter is fine."

"I hear a but in that sentence."

"I do have some concerns about her mental wellbeing. Aaliyah has suffered a tremendous loss, so it's understandable she's very emotional right now. Having the support of her family is going to make all the difference," the doctor said, standing up from the chair. "Mrs. Mills, I enjoyed speaking with you but I must go check on my other patients. Please, go see your daughter and I'll be back to check on her shortly."

"Thank you, Doctor Blanton."

Precious remained seated for a few more minutes, wanting to put on her bravest face before entering Aaliyah's hospital room. What she learned was even worse than she'd imagined. Her daughter's husband and unborn child were both taken from her at the same time. Precious didn't know how Aaliyah would survive such devastation but she would be by her side every step of the way.

$$$

When Genesis arrived at the bi-level home on Cardinal Dr. in Poughkeepsie, New York, he was baffled as to why Nico was being so secretive and wanted to meet way out here. He walked on the paver stone walkway towards the older modeled ranch style house. Lorenzo was waiting for Genesis before he even made it to the door.

"I should've known you would be here too," Genesis said stepping inside. "Why are we here and where's Nico?" he asked, sounding agitated.

"We didn't want to say too much until you were here in person. Between Arnez and Maverick, we tryna be as cautious as possible," Lorenzo said, closing the door.

"I get it but we couldn't meet someplace closer? I don't like being so far away from Genevieve."

"I understand, we all do but..." Lorenzo stopped talking when he realized someone else had Genesis's attention.

"Miss Meka! You're alive." Genesis hurried over to the older lady who'd been working with them for years and hugged her tightly. "We all thought you were dead. How long have you known she was alive?" he asked Nico.

"Last night she showed up at my house. I brought her here this morning. I wanted to get her out of New York until we get all this shit dealt with," Nico said.

"Whose house is this and Miss Meka what happened. Sit down and tell me everything," Genesis said, holding her hand as they walked over to the couch.

"This is my grandmother's house," Nico stated. "When she died years ago, she left this house to me. I keep it for sentimental reasons. No one knows about it, so I thought this would be the perfect place for Miss Meka to stay, until everything is resolved."

"I told Nico I don't think Maverick is coming back for me. If he wanted me dead, then he would've killed me when he had the chance," Miss Meka spoke up, still visibly shaken by what happened.

"Tell me everything that happened with Maverick," Genesis wanted to know.

"I arrived to work early in the morning like I normally do. Two men grabbed me the second I put my key in the door. They must've been waiting for me."

"I'm sure it was Raymond's talkin' ass who hipped Maverick to all the shit he knew," Lorenzo popped.

"No doubt," Genesis agreed. "So then what happened, Miss Meka?"

"After the two men brought me in the office building, the man Maverick came in a few seconds later. That's when..." Miss Meka became choked up and her eyes teared up.

"It's okay, Miss Meka. Take your time." Genesis gently rubbed her arm.

"He put a gun to my head and forced me to send those text messages to all of you. I didn't want to," she cried.

"Did Maverick hurt you?" Genesis asked.

"Not physically. He just scared me. He was cold but then once he took me to some other location, he turned into a different person."

"Different how?"

"He wanted to make sure I was comfortable. He even apologized for how I was treated at the office and for threatening me."

"I'm just relieved he didn't kill her," Nico let out a deep breath.

"It wasn't by accident," Miss Meka said in a low voice.

Nico, Genesis and Lorenzo all turned to Miss Meka, wondering what she meant by that. They waited for her to elaborate on the statement until Lorenzo grew impatient.

"Do you know the reason Maverick didn't kill you?" Lorenzo asked.

"Yes, because of you Genesis."

"Me…why me?"

"He said he was letting me live because you didn't kill his mother."

"That nigga make me sick!" Nico spit. "Now he wants us to think he's some fuckin' martyr. Sonofabitch," he fumed.

"Did Maverick tell you anything else?" Genesis asked Miss Meka.

She nodded her head yes before continuing. "After he held me at some house for a week, he dropped me off in the city and gave me some money for a taxi. Before he left, Maverick told me to give you a message."

"What's the message?" Genesis was starting to feel like he was playing chess with a ghost as an opponent.

"He repaid the favor by letting me live and now the two of you are even. But he's coming for each of you and everyone you love, one person at a time," Miss Meka revealed.

"Man, I'm too old for this shit," Nico scoffed.

"Nico, you say that same bullshit every year," Lorenzo cracked.

"And I mean it every year too but ya' motherfuckers just keep pulling me back in."

"So, it's our fault?" Lorenzo mocked.

"That's what the fuck I said and I'm stickin' to it."

"I'm really tired. Do you mind if I excuse myself, and go lay down?" Miss Meka asked Genesis.

"Of course. Please, go get some rest," Genesis said, taking her hand, to help her up. Miss Meka was a little petite lady with a head full of gray hair, that she always wore in a low bun. No one would ever believe that such a sweet looking older lady, had been working for three of the biggest drug kingpins on the east coast, for all these years.

"I'll come and check on you before I leave," Nico told Miss Meka. "But that won't be until the security team arrives."

'I'm sorry you had to get involved in this mess," Genesis looked down at Miss Meka and said. "If you need anything you let me know." He hugged her one last time before she headed to the bedroom down the hall.

"On a positive note, Miss Meka is alive and

well," Lorenzo announced in an upbeat tone to kill the somber vibe. "Seriously, I know you the guilt was tearing you up inside, when you thought she was dead. You can let that go now, Genesis."

"I can't let shit go until Maverick and Arnez are both dead," Genesis sat back down and said. "I didn't think I would ever want to get out the game. This shit run through my veins so deep, I figured I wouldn't retire until I was an old man. Even then, I would be fighting to stay in the race. But now..." Genesis's voice trailed off.

"I think we're all starting to feel that way," Lorenzo acknowledged. "I mean when shit is good, it's great but when it goes bad, the nightmare don't ever seem to end."

"When I look at someone like Miss Meka and I see the fear in her eyes. Then I have to try and rationalize how my choices almost cost her, her life," Genesis said, battling with his conscious." I was this close to taking Maverick's mother's life. That shit fucks wit' me. Killing other sinners in this game, ain't neva bothered me. It's part of the risk you take, when you sign up for this fast life. But it's the innocent ones, that's making me question, if this is the life I want to continue to live."

After all these years, Genesis had finally

come to the fork in the road. He no longer knew which path he wanted to choose. Or maybe he would let life, choose it for him.

Chapter Nineteen

Motives

Stand up niggas, we only ducking indictments. Dope boys, off-white, looking like soft white on 'em. You know what I'm sayin'? We in the building, we came for a billion. Ain't nobody playin'! Caleb rhymed along to the Jay-Z verse on Talk Up, while the club was going crazy as the song blasted from the speakers.

"Yo, this the best birthday party ever!" Floyd was hyped, drinking champagne straight out the bottle, doing his two step dance move.

"Yeah, I'm having a good time too," Caleb

nodded, standing up in a VIP skybox looking down at the crowd.

"You showed out!" Prevan smiled, putting his hand on Caleb's shoulder. "You did good, bro!"

"Man, I was wondering when you was gon' get here." Caleb gave his brother a hug. "Here, take a bottle and celebrate wit' us," he said handing Prevan some champagne.

"Happy Birthday, Caleb."

Caleb turned and saw it was Prevan's baby mama Celinda sending him birthday wishes. "Why the fuck you bring this bird to my party?" Caleb barked to his brother.

"Nigga what!" Celinda folded her arms and rolled her neck. Then she started cursing him out in Spanish.

"Both of you relax!" Prevan put his hands between them.

"How you gon' defend him against me! I'm ya' girlfriend!" Celinda spat.

"Yo, will you chill!" Prevan spit back.

"Celinda, come sit down with me," Mia said, grabbing her sister's arm.

"Man, what tha fuck is wrong wit' you. I told you that broad had been fuckin' that nigga Mack and he was tryna have me killed."

"I spoke to Celinda bout that shit. She only started messing around wit' him when she thought we had broken up but she swear she had no idea he was planning on killin' you," Prevan insisted.

"If yo' dumbass wanna believe that shit, that's on you. But keep her snake ass away from me. Cause I swear on everything, if I even think that broad is tryna fuck me over again, she gets no warnings. It's a fuckin' wrap for her," Caleb promised.

"Calm down, Caleb. You talkin' crazy right now. Celinda is the mother of my child…your niece."

"And it's the only reason, that grimey bitch ain't dead yet. So keep her ass away from me. I'm serious!" Caleb jabbed his finger in his brother's chest. "She's a snake and if you keep fuckin' around wit' her, you gon' end up dead or back in jail," he warned. "I'm done wit' this conversation. This my party and I ain't lettin' that bird kill my vibe."

Prevan didn't know how to respond to what his brother said, so only thing he could do was walk away.

"Do you think you were too hard on yo' brother?" Floyd asked.

"Fuck no!" Caleb scowled. "One thing I've

learned from being in this game, is an un loyal muthafucker within yo' circle, is more dangerous than yo' enemy. That's my brother and I love 'em but I ain't bout to die, cause he sprung on a sorry ass hoe."

"Caleb, can I speak to you for a minute."

"What is it, Mia?" he snapped

"I was just checking to make sure you were okay. I didn't want my sister to ruin your party?"

"I'm good." Caleb kept it short. "Anything else?"

"I did want to give you this," Mia said nervously. Caleb looked down and saw she had a present. "I got you a birthday gift." Mia handed the small wrapped box to him.

"You didn't have to do this, Mia," Caleb said, feeling guilty he had been so dismissive towards her.

"I wanted to. I know you have everything now and it's nothing fancy but I hope you like it," she said sweetly.

"I'm sure I will. Thank you," Caleb smiled.

"Okay, well I won't keep you. Happy Birthday, Caleb."

"See, that's the type of chick you need," Floyd said. after Mia had walked off.

"Mia's a cool chick and maybe if she wasn't

related to Celinda, I would consider dating her but..."

"Don't punish Mia for that. She can't help who her sister is, that's on they mama."

"Nigga, you so stupid," Caleb laughed.

"I'm serious. That girl love you. She would treat you right and you wouldn't have to worry about her runnin' these streets and doin' dumb shit."

"Yo, look who just walked in!" Caleb flashed his million dollar smile, paying no attention to all the endorsing Floyd was doing for Mia. "Damn, and she look so fuckin' gorgeous too."

Shiffon was standing underneath one of the bright lights near the dance floor. The emerald green mini dress with gold studs, accentuating the double spaghetti straps, deep v neckline and studded trim, had her standing out in a club full of bad bitches.

"Don't go chasing after her!" Floyd called out, trying to stop Caleb from bailing the VIP area to get Shiffon but he was gone.

When Caleb got downstairs, he observed Shiffon for a couple minutes, wanting to see how she conducted herself amongst thirsty niggas with money. She looked like a tempting piece of candy, standing all alone and dudes were flocking to her like bees to honey. Shiffon maintained her composure and politely brushed off every one of her pursuers, while gazing around the club in search of Caleb.

"You've just made my entire night," Caleb snuck up from behind Shiffon and announced.

"There you are!" Shiffon beamed.

"I didn't think you were coming," Caleb admitted.

"I wasn't sure I would be able to but I got back in town this morning, so it worked out. Here," Shiffon continued to smile handing Caleb a gift. "I got this for you."

"Another surprise. Not only do you show up to my birthday party but you come wit' a gift. Thank you." Caleb leaned in and kissed Shiffon on the cheek. The gesture was so sweet, Shiffon couldn't' help but blush.

From a short distance, Maverick scrutinized the interaction between Caleb and Shiffon. There was a combination of rage and lust while dissecting each movement she made. It took every ounce of strength Maverick had, not to step to the woman he was positive seduced him, before killing members of his crew.

"Is that her? Is she one of the strippers you hired for Klay's birthday party?" Micah questioned.

"She doesn't have all the heavy makeup on and she isn't wearing that wig but ain't no doubt in my mind, it's her for sure," Maverick said, thinking how she was even prettier with the softer makeup and her natural hair.

"Cool. Let's get outta here before they see us," Micah said, putting down his drink and heading towards the exit.

Maverick lingered behind for a moment, continuing to stare at Shiffon and Caleb. *Yeah, enjoy your evening lovely, cause life as you know it, is about to come to an end,* Maverick thought to himself before finally leaving out.

Also observing the pair was a heartbroken Mia. "Who is that woman Caleb is talking to?" she asked Floyd, who wasn't a fan of the potential coupling.

"Just some woman Caleb does business with."

"The way he has his hands all over her, it doesn't seem like just some woman to me. He's never touched me like that."

"Mia, I know you really like Caleb and I think he likes you too. You just have to give him some time. He's young...you know," Floyd said, trying to give Mia a glimmer of hope, she had a chance with Caleb.

The longer Mia observed the interaction between Caleb and Shiffon, the more her glimmer of hope dimmed. It was obvious Caleb was completely enamored with the beauty and from where Mia was standing, the woman seemed to be smitten with Caleb too. The typically shy and reserved young lady, felt a burning sensation bubbling deep within, that she had never felt before. Mia's feelings towards Caleb was more than a teenage crush. She wanted him to be her man and if Caleb was drawn to women like Shiffon, then Mia was prepared to step her seduction game all the way up.

$$$

"Where's Aaliyah? I wanna see her!" Nico brushed past Precious, not even giving her a chance to open the door all the way.

"Nico, slow down!" Precious yelled out, closing the door. "Aaliyah is upstairs sleeping. Let her rest."

"I want to see my daughter," Nico demanded.

"Fine. You can go see her but don't wake her up. Do you hear me, Nico!"

Nico ignored Precious and stormed off

to see Aaliyah. He ran up the spiral staircase and down the long hallway until reaching her bedroom. When he looked in on his daughter, she was sleeping peacefully. There was no sign, of all the trauma she'd recently endured. Nico wanted to run to Aaliyah's bedside and hold her but he knew Precious was right, their daughter needed to rest.

"What took you so long to call me?!" Nico snapped when he came back downstairs, into the living room where Precious was sitting.

"Don't yell at me!" Precious snapped back. "Like I told you on the phone, I was in Miami trying to keep Aaliyah from having a nervous breakdown. Calling you wasn't a priority, my daughter was."

"Our daughter and if you called me, I could've come to Miami to help you."

"Help how? Were you going to miraculously bring Dale back to life and make Aaliyah pregnant again. No! So stop complaining and just be grateful I was able to bring her back home."

"I apologize." Nico walked over to the window and put his head down. "Knowing I was going to be a grandfather, has been the only thing I've had to look forward to lately."

"I know what you mean. I was looking

forward to being a grandmother too. But we can't think about our disappointments right now. Our daughter is in trouble."

Nico looked up and turned to face Precious. "I'm not following you. I thought the doctor said she was okay?"

"Physically yes but mentally, I've never seen her so broken. I remember when I lost my baby and then right after I got out the hospital, I believed I had lost Supreme too. I was completely numb," Precious said, becoming emotional thinking back to that time in her life. It was uncomfortable for Nico to listen to since he was the one responsible for Precious losing her child.

"I can't pretend to completely understand what you went through but we have to believe Aaliyah will survive just like you did."

"The only reason I survived was because I was on a mission to find the person who killed Supreme. I was consumed with it, so I wasn't able to fall into some deep depression. I was driven by revenge and murder. But this...this is too much for Aaliyah to handle." Tears began to fall down Precious's face.

"Precious, please don't cry." Nico came over and held the mother of his first born child. "Aaliyah is strong. She'll get through this. We'll do everything possible to make sure that happens."

"I pray you're right because I can't lose her. She's still my baby and when Aaliyah hurts, I hurt too. I feel her pain and I'm so afraid she won't be able to let it go."

Chapter Twenty

Can't Have Everything

Caleb was on his way to check on one of his distribution spots when he saw the unknown call pop up on his screen. He had a feeling it was nobody but Arnez.

"Hello."

"Can you talk?"

"I wouldn't of answered the phone if I couldn't," Caleb said, as he whipped through traffic. "I ain't heard nothing from you since I gave you the dude Micah's number."

"Yeah, I've been getting things together, so I

can get back to Philly."

"Really, when do you think you'll be here?" It was the main reason Caleb even answered the phone. He needed to know when Arnez would be back, so he could kill him.

"Soon but in the meantime I have something for you to do and I need it done immediately," Arnez stated.

Caleb locked his jaw, sick of Arnez ordering him around like he was his personal do boy. He wanted this shit to be over and the only way that would be possible is if Arnez was dead.

"What you need?" Caleb asked, trying to sound like he was down for whatever.

"I need for you to kill Genesis." Caleb damn near crashed into a semi-trailer truck when Arnez made his proclamation. "Are you there?" he questioned when he didn't hear a response from Caleb.

"Yeah...yeah, I'm here. A car almost cut me off, so I had to pull over," Caleb lied, ready to jump through the phone and choke Arnez up.

"Oh, okay. So umm did you hear what I said."

"Yep. How do you expect for me to pull this off? Genesis always has armed bodyguards wit' him."

"Not at night when he's at home with his wife

and child. You'll call Genesis late at night and tell him there's an emergency but you can't tell him over the phone. He'll ask you what's it about and you simply say my name. He'll be rushing for you to get to his house."

"What about his wife? I'm sure Genesis will mention it's me at the door when I come over late that night."

"Then kill Talisa too. I'm sure she'll rather be dead if her cherished Genesis is no longer with her," Arnez mocked, with a sinister laugh.

"I don't think you've thought this through. Why the rush to have me kill Genesis?"

"Because it's time for him to die and I'll never gain access to Genesis again but you can and you will or else."

"Or else what...you makin' threats now?"

"I shouldn't have to since everything you have is because of me. I brought you into the fold. Took you from being a low on the totem pole worker for Khyree to dominating the Philly drug game. It was me that made you. Don't make me break you too," Arnez warned.

"No need for things to get ugly. We both have the same goal...to get what we want. You want Genesis dead and I want to be the king of this shit," Caleb stated.

"I'm glad we're on the same page. I would hate for you to lose your sweet mother, niece and brother because of your loyalty to Genesis. Does his life mean more to you than your own family?"

"Arnez, there's no need for you to threaten my family. We have a deal and I'ma stick to it. If Genesis has to die, then so be it."

"I knew you were smart, Caleb. I'll give you thirty days to get this done and not a day more. After that, for each day you're late, one of your family members will die, starting with your mother. I'll be in touch."

This time, Caleb really did have to pull over after Arnez hung up. He was ready to put his fist through the windshield, he was so enraged. This wasn't how Caleb imagined things playing out but now Arnez had his back against the wall. He had to make a choice and whatever decision Caleb made, it wouldn't be in his favor.

$$$

"You're up early," Precious smiled when she saw Supreme in the kitchen making a protein shake. "I was upset when I woke up and I wasn't in your arms," she said, giving him a kiss.

"I didn't really sleep too good last night. I

thought maybe if I went for a run this morning, I might feel a little better," Supreme said, pulling Precious closer for another kiss.

"I'm assuming the business you're doing with Genesis is still not resolved," Precious commented while pouring a glass of orange juice.

"Far from it but that isn't the reason I didn't sleep good."

"Then what is it?"

"Aaliyah. She seemed to be making improvements the last week or so but yesterday when I got home, I went up to her room to talk and she wanted to be left alone. I'm worried she might be backtracking."

"She has been doing a lot better but we have to be prepared, that she might be hit with this cloud of sadness at any time," Precious said.

"Good morning!" Aaliyah popped up in the kitchen unexpectedly, catching Supreme and Precious off guard. Although they were both pleased she seemed extra bubbly.

"Good morning to you!" they both exclaimed simultaneously.

"How did you sleep last night?" Precious asked, walking over to Aaliyah, stroking her hair.

"I slept great. I woke up feeling energized. Dad, are you going for a run?" she asked, noticing how he was dressed.

"Sure am, after I finish my drink."

"Do you mind if I join you?"

"Of course not. I would love to go running with my favorite daughter," Supreme smiled.

"Dad, I'm your only daughter."

"True but you're still my favorite." They both laughed.

"Let me get dressed and throw on my running shoes. I'll be right back." Aaliyah hurried off, leaving Precious and Supreme to eye each other excitedly.

"Wow! What a difference a day makes," Precious beamed. "For the first time in weeks, I saw a glimpse of my magnificent daughter. She's back!"

"It did feel pretty good when she asked to join me for my run. She was probably in her feelings yesterday but after having a good night sleep, woke up being back to Aaliyah again," Supreme reasoned.

"Exactly," Precious agreed. "She really has been doing so much better. Like I said, there will be bad days but as long as there are more good, than bad...we're winning."

Supreme and Precious held each other for a long embrace, rejoicing over their daughter's progress. Seeing the old Aaliyah coming back, gave them the courage they needed to keep the faith.

Chapter Twenty-One

Only A Matter Of Time

"You've had our men watching homegirl for the last few weeks but you haven't said when you want them to make their move," Cam questioned Maverick.

"I'll let you know when it's time," Maverick said, flipping through the pictures one of his men had taken of Shiffon while she's been under surveillance.

"What are you waiting for?" Cam pressed.

"Mind yo' business, Cam. You have enough to deal wit'. Like making sure the trap is set for

Genesis and his people. We have to make sure that shit goes accordingly. Let me worry about Shiffon."

As Maverick continued looking over the images of Shiffon, he knew it was a stroke of luck that he was even able to find her. When Micah told him Arnez sent one of his workers to get in touch with him, he thought nothing of it until he said the workers name was Caleb. He specifically remembered, Raymond mentioned a dude named Caleb who worked for Genesis, was the person who hired the woman that set him up. Maverick knew that couldn't be a coincidence and once he spoke to Arnez, his suspicions were confirmed. It turned out to be an added bonus when Shiffon showed up at Caleb's birthday party. Maverick figured Caleb would lead him to the mystery woman but not so soon. Now that he had her every move being tracked, Maverick was taking his time figuring out how he planned to deal with her.

$$$

"Genevieve finally fell asleep. I think she was trying to stay up because she enjoys when I sing to her," Talisa giggled, taking off her bathrobe. "Do you want me to get you anything from the kitchen before I take a shower?" she asked Genesis.

"No, I'm good babe." Genesis sprinkled kisses on Talisa's shoulder. "You're so good with her. Thank you for being you."

"Thank you for trusting me to take care of your daughter. I know how special she is to you."

"And so are you. Hold on one sec, babe. Let me take this call."

"Okay. When you're done with your call, come join me in the shower." Talisa blew Genesis a kiss, before disappearing to the master bath.

Genesis smiled and mouthed I love you to Talisa, right before speaking into his phone. "Hello."

"Hey Genesis, it's me, Caleb."

"Yeah, I know. I saw your number. What's going on? I'm surprised you're calling so late."

"It's an emergency. I really need to speak with you. In person if possible."

"You're here in New York?" surprised Caleb wasn't in Philly.

"Yes."

"This can't wait until the morning?" Genesis questioned.

"No. It's really important. It's about Arnez."

"Say no more. Come on over."

"A'ight, I'll be there in a few," Caleb said hanging up.

Genesis had given everyone strict instructions not discuss potential incriminating information over the phone. His lawyer had warned him, that although he had been released from jail and the charges against him had been dropped, thanks to Lorenzo and T-Roc making sure the government's snitch had been permanently dealt with, he was still on their watch list. Genesis was trying not to take any chances.

"Baby, are you coming to join me?" Talisa called out. "This shower isn't the same without you."

Genesis reluctantly went into the bathroom to let Talisa know he wouldn't be joining her. Seeing her naked body through glass of the shower door, in the midst of all that steam, made Genesis second guess his decision but only for a second.

"As bad as I want to get in the shower with you, I have some unexpected business to deal with," Genesis explained.

"This late? What business do you need to handle this time of night?"

"I don't know all the details but Caleb is on his way over. It's probably gonna take a minute."

"Okay. I'm exhausted but I'll try to stay up, so you can put me to sleep," Talisa teased.

"I like the sound of that."

Genesis was tempted to walk over and give his wife a quick kiss before leaving out but he knew that one kiss would lead to so much more. Instead he said, "Love you."

"Love you too," Talisa replied sweetly.

"Damn, when Caleb said he'll be here in a few, he wasn't lying," Genesis said out loud when he heard the doorbell ringing. While heading to the door, numerous thoughts filled his head. He wondered what was so urgent, it couldn't wait until tomorrow. *Caleb said he needed to see me about Arnez. I had no idea Caleb even knew anything about Arnez, except for what I told him after Genevieve was kidnapped. Even then I kept the information limited. I told him Arnez was responsible for my daughter's kidnapping but not our long history of being sworn enemies. I'm intrigued to find out what Caleb might know.* Genesis thought, right before opening the door.

$$$

"Aaliyah, what are you doing?" Precious was stunned when she walked into her daughter's bedroom and she was packing her clothes.

"I decided it was time for me to move out and get my own place," Aaliyah said, while she continued packing her clothes.

"Your own place...don't you think it's way too soon for that?"

"No, honestly I think it's long overdue. I've been staying here for over two months. I need to have my own space."

"We live on an estate. This house has nothing but space...too much of it. We could literally not see each other ever, if we didn't want to. Space isn't a reason for you to leave. I really want you to stay, Aaliyah," Precious pleaded.

"Mother, it means the world to me, you want me to be here but the longer I stay, the more I'm using you and dad as a crutch. Plus, I really want to move back to the city. Living in New Jersey has been great. Laying by the pool, playing tennis, walking through the gardens and just being surrounded by love, has been so therapeutic. But I miss the hustle and bustle of the city life."

"Aaliyah, I'm thrilled you're ready to get back to living your life," Precious said, sitting down on the edge of the bed, where her daughter was packing. "You've come so far. You're not even the same person I saw in the hospital all those weeks ago."

"Then what's the problem?"

"I think you're moving too fast. I'm afraid if..."

"If what? If I don't let you keep a watchful eye on me, I'll fall into some deep depression and kill myself?" Aaliyah's accusatory tone made Precious uneasy. "I'm not some weak child, Mother."

"I never said that you were?"

"Well that's how you're acting. Like I need you to hold my hand. Newsflash, I don't! I'm capable of taking care of myself."

"Aaliyah, I apologize if I upset you. That's not my intention. I'm worried. Isn't it okay for a mother to worry about her child?" Precious laid her hands on top of Aaliyah's, to stop her from packing and instead listen. "Losing Dale and the baby is still fresh. You need more time to get over it."

"I'll never get over it...never! And living in this house won't make it better either. It's time for me to leave." Aaliyah wasn't budging.

"I don't agree but I respect your decision. Instead of staying in some hotel in the city, how about I help you find a really fabulous apartment," Precious suggested.

"I'm not staying at a hotel. I already found a beautiful renovated townhouse in Harlem."

"Wow! Talk about moving fast. I had no idea you were even looking and you've already gotten a place." Precious took a deep breath because she was never good at biting her tongue but she didn't want Aaliyah to shut down. She knew her daughter better than anyone and if she didn't choose her words carefully, this conversation would turn vicious very quickly.

"Yes, I've been wanting to move out for a while now, I was simply waiting until I found the perfect place and I did," Aaliyah assured her.

"I'm happy for you. Well, at least let your mother help you pick out furniture and decorate."

"That's been handled too," Aaliyah said, zipping up her suitcase.

Precious stared at Aaliyah who was dressed casually in some cut off short a tank top and flip flops. It seemed like yesterday, she was wearing her favorite pink dress with matching barrettes in her hair. Aaliyah would go on and on about how her ponytails had to be just right. At this moment, Precious would give anything to go back to those days when she was a little girl because something didn't feel right. She couldn't put her finger on it but a mother knows and Precious had a bad feeling there was another reason why Aaliyah was anxious to move out.

"Are you sure there's nothing I can do to help?"

"Mother, I have everything covered," Aaliyah insisted. "When I'm settled into my new place, I'll invite you over. I promise," she said giving Precious a hug.

"You're leaving now, at this very moment... don't you want to wait for your father to get home to say goodbye?"

"I'm not moving to Paris," Aaliyah laughed. "And this isn't goodbye, it's I'll see you later," she smiled. "Don't worry about me. I'll be fine." Aaliyah kissed her mother and off she went. Precious wanted to tackle her daughter and make her stay but knew it would only delay the inevitable. Instead she stood at the top of the stairwell, overlooking the foyer and watched in dismay as Aaliyah walked out the door.

Chapter Twenty-Two

Secrets Unlocked

Shiffon was leaving The Bellevue Philadelphia after being pampered at Artur Kirsh Salon & Spa, doing a little shopping and getting a light bite to eat with a ton of drinks at the Palm Bar. To say she was tipsy was an understatement. If she had gotten pulled over by the police, she would've most definitely failed a breathalyzer. But it was the first time Shiffon had a break, from her hectic career as a highly sought after assassin in a very long time. With the level of stress her job entailed, she relished being able to put her guard down and relaxing.

"One second, let me find what you need," Shiffon giggled to the valet, while searching in her purse for the ticket.

"I think it's in your hand," he said, noticing how inebriated she was.

"You're absolutely right," Shiffon giggled some more. "Don't judge me. I'm having a blond moment," she said handing him her ticket.

"No problem. I'll be right back with your car."

While waiting for the valet to return with her vehicle, Shiffon debated whether she should call for an Uber. Eventually she decided against it, believing she could handle being behind the wheel of the car.

"Thanks," Shiffon smiled, giving the valet a nice tip and driving off. She had no choice but to turn right on the one way street and without warning a car stopped in the front, blocking her in. Shiffon waited for a few seconds and when the car didn't move she blew her horn. "What the fuck?!" she shouted out the window. A few seconds later when a black minivan pulled up, blocking her from behind, Ring The Alarm started playing in her head.

Shiffon was drunk not dumb. She reached in the hidden compartment to retrieve her gun.

"I'm not the bitch for you muthafuckas to be tryna rob," she barked, ready to bust a cap. But her take no prisoners fury, quickly shifted to fear. "No! No! No!" Shiffon yelled, realizing her gun was gone. "That fuckin' valet!" It was then she knew this wasn't some random robbery, it was a setup.

Fear and being panic stricken, made Shiffon snap out her drunken stupor and sober up quick. Dealing with limited options, she pressed her foot down on the gas, trying to force some space between the cars so she could make a U-turn. It seemed like a good idea and it might've worked if three men didn't get out the car, carrying baseball bats. When she realized they were going to bash the windows to drag her out the car, Shiffon ducked down to keep the broken glass from cutting up her face.

"Where the fuck you think you going!" the bulky man roared, sticking his hand in the car and unlocking the driver's door.

"What the fuck do you want!" Shiffon shouted, as she was being dragged out the car.

"You!" He roared tossing her in the back of the minivan, where she was blindfolded and tied up as the minivan drove off. During her ride, Shiffon started thinking about all the people she's crossed and which one was able to track her down. For someone who had killed so many, Shiffon was scared to die.

When the minivan stopped and the back door opened, Shiffon was prepared to feel the burning sensation from the bullets ripping through the flesh of her body. She even said a silent prayer, hoping God would show her forgiveness for all her sins. Shiffon wasn't ready to die but was prepared for the inevitable as the tears flowed.

"I didn't know killers could cry," Maverick taunted, taking off her blindfold.

"Not you," Shiffon mumbled, wishing it was anybody but him seeking retribution.

"I guess that means you remember me."

Those lips, those eyes, how could I ever forget you, Shiffon thought to herself, remembering how attracted she had been to Maverick on the night they met. She wasn't expecting to catch feelings but it didn't matter, she had a job to do and Shiffon was always a professional when it came to an assignment.

"Yes, I do."

"Good. It was important to me, you knew who was about to kill you," Maverick smiled and said, slamming the door shut.

$$$

Precious woke up, once again thinking about Aaliyah. She reached for her phone to give her a call but stopped herself. She had been calling her multiple times a day since she left and the last thing she wanted to be was the annoying mother.

"I'm gonna try something a little bit different," Precious got out of bed and said, heading towards Supreme's office. When she reached the middle of the stairs, she could hear her husband yelling.

"Fuck!" Supreme tossed down his phone, letting out a deep sigh.

"Baby, what's wrong. What has you so upset?"

"Everything," he threw his hands up in the air and yelled.

"You seem more on edge than me, so my idea should be great for both of us."

"What idea?"

"Let's take the private jet and relax at that island resort I love so much for a couple days. It will help us both relieve some of this stress," Precious suggested.

"I can't go out of town right now," Supreme griped. "There's just too much going on."

"Business can wait for a couple days."

"No it can't. Genesis is still missing."

"Genesis is missing? That's news to me!" Precious gasped.

"We were keeping it under wraps, thinking it was nothing major but now we know it's bad."

"Oh gosh, this can't be happening. Genevieve can't lose her mother and her father," Precious bawled.

"Don't even go there. Skylar might pull through and you damn sure can't count Genesis out."

"True. Genesis is resourceful."

"Yes, he is but we need our whole team on this and now T-Roc has to go to Miami because some fuckin' crazy person, kidnapped his grandson. I understand wanting to be there for Justina but this is not the time for a fuckin' family emergency! Genesis needs us."

"Wait a minute. Somebody kidnapped Justina's baby. I had no ideas she'd even given birth."

"Me neither but with everything going on with Aaliyah, her losing her baby. T-Roc probably felt it would be insensitive for him to celebrate being a new grandfather, in front of me and Nico. I do feel horrible for what happened to him and his family but we still need to focus on finding out where Genesis is."

Precious felt like she wanted to vomit. *Dear God, please don't let what I'm thinking be true*, she said to herself.

"Babe, are you okay?" Supreme walked over to his wife, who looked like all the color had been drained from her face.

"I'm fine, just feeling a little light headed. I slept late and I still haven't eaten," she said sitting down.

"Well come on, let's go get you something to eat." Supreme reached out his hand to Precious.

"I'm actually meeting Aaliyah in the city for lunch. I'll grab a quick snack before I leave."

"Are you sure?"

"Baby, I'm positive. I'm just hungry, that's all," Precious laughed. "You focus on finding Genesis."

"Speaking of Genesis, Amir just sent me a text. I have to go meet him. He said he has news."

"Then go."

"Are you sure you're going to be okay?"

"If something was wrong, I would tell you... now go!" Precious said kissing Supreme goodbye.

"Okay. Give my love to Aaliyah. I'll see you when I get back home."

The moment Supreme was out the door,

Precious rushed upstairs to get dressed. She was determined to get to the truth, no matter what direction it took her in. Precious knew Aaliyah was being secretive and was hiding something but never did she imagine it could be anything this ominous.

Chapter Twenty-Three

Streets Is Done

"This used to be my spot, until it got shut down," Caleb commented to Arnez, looking around at the Graffiti Pier.

"It doesn't look closed to me. I guess you can say, rules are meant to be broken, even legal ones," Arnez cracked, finding humor in his own joke.

"Who am I to argue about that, since I'm a drug dealer. I move dope but we're not here to discuss that. I did what you asked." Caleb said, edging closer to Arnez.

"His partners are trying to keep it hush hush

but word on the streets is the great Genesis Taylor is dead. I hear Talisa made it out alive. How did that happen?"

"When I came to meet Genesis, he didn't want to discuss business at his penthouse, so we left. Little did he know that decision saved his wife's life," Caleb explained.

"I did have another question...where's the body?"

"Hopefully, at the bottom of the Hudson River."

"Caleb! Look at you," Arnez grinned widely. "I gotta admit, I wasn't sure you'd pull it off. You hid it well but I could see how much you admired Genesis and wanted to be like him. I didn't think you'd be able to look your idol in the eyes and kill him."

"I guess you thought wrong," Caleb said smugly. "I'm assuming that means our business is finally done."

"You've served your purpose." Arnez patted Caleb on his shoulder. "You did, what I was never able to do...kill Genesis. I'm proud of you."

"Listen, I gotta go. I have a drug empire to run. Not sure, where you headed next and honestly I don't want to know nor do I care. Just stay the fuck out my life," Caleb nodded.

"Arrogance looks good on you kid. I always knew you'd go far in this cutthroat game called dope dealing. Glad to know I was right but I usually am," Arnez bragged.

"Not this time, muthafucka." Genesis stepped out of the dark shadow. "You can't always be right and don't even think about reaching for yo' piece, or I'ma blow your fuckin' hand off."

"You sonofabitch!" Arnez roared at Caleb. "I made you king and this is how you repay me, by aligning yourself wit' my fuckin' enemy. I shoulda killed you," he raged.

"But you didn't. The fact you ever thought, I would cross Genesis for yo' sick ass, should let you know, yo' time is up. I'll leave you to handle this Genesis. You deserve to be the one to put a bullet in this fuckin' monster." Caleb stepped back and Genesis moved forward.

"I almost don't wanna pull the trigger just yet. I'm gettin' more gratification at the thought of watching you die."

"Fuck you, Genesis! I'ma die a happy man, knowing Maverick is gonna pick up, right where I left off. You think I'm a monster, you've met your match wit' him." Arnez winked his eye, and gave his devilish smile, trying to take one last jab at his archenemy.

"Enjoy dancing wit' the devil, you snake ass nigga!" Genesis emptied his clip, leaving one in the chamber. He took great satisfaction as Arnez's bloody body fell face up in a murky puddle of water. Vengeance had finally been served.

$$$

When Precious pulled up to the brownstone on Park Avenue, she took a deep breath and mentally prepared herself for the finessing she was about to do. She touched up her lipstick, fluffed her hair before exiting out her car.

"Precious, what are you doing here?" Chantal questioned, when she opened her front door, with a bewildered glare on her face.

"I came over to see how you're doing." Chantal continued to give Precious the same baffled stare. "Supreme told me what happened to Justina. I'm so sorry."

"Oh please, you can't stand my daughter and you hate me even worse," Chantal sniped, ready to slam the door in Precious's face.

"Wait!" Precious put her hand up to keep the door from shutting.

"I'm not going to stand here and listen to you gloat over my family's misfortune."

"Chantal, I would never do that. When I heard about what happened to Justina, it hit a nerve. Our daughters grew up together. We've had our differences but we're both mothers and I understand your pain."

"Come in," Chantal said, still weary of Precious's sudden kind gesture.

"Thank you."

"Can I get you something to drink?" Chantal offered.

"A glass of wine but only if you'll join me."

"Two glasses of wine coming up," Chantal beamed, always looking for an excuse to have a drink.

After an hour or so of small talk and Precious stroking Chantal's ego, she felt it's was time to circle back to the real reason she showed up at the door, of a woman she couldn't stand.

"Supreme mentioned T-Roc was going to Miami to see Justina. I'm surprised you didn't go with him."

"T-Roc can be so controlling." Chantal rolled her eyes, sipping on her third or fourth glass of wine. Precious had lost count, as she was still babysitting her first one. "Of course I wanted to go be with my daughter but T-Roc insisted I stay here."

"Why is that?"

"My husband tends to think I can be over dramatic. He said with Justina already being so traumatized, me being there would just make things worse. He said I can go in a couple of days, after he's done playing hero," Chantal said sarcastically.

"Poor Justina. No mother deserves this. Do you know exactly when you're grandson was kidnapped?"

"Of course! I'll never forget when Justina called me in the middle of the night, completely frantic. It was July 11th. She was beside herself. Luckily, T-Roc was home that night and not out with one of his mistresses. He was able to calm Justina down. He's a terrible husband but he is a great father. I have to admit, our son and daughter adore him," she shrugged.

"Do the police have any leads?"

"No! Although the nanny has suspiciously gone missing. No one has seen or heard from her since my sweet grandson disappeared." Chantal's eyes watered up. "Whoever did this, will have hell to pay. They'll either end up dead or rot in prison for the rest of their life."

"Hopefully they'll catch him soon," Precious said.

"You think it's a man too? So do I!" Chantal exclaimed. "I told T-Roc that only a man could do something so bold and cruel."

"I agree."

"I wasn't going to mention it but since we're bonding as mothers, I'm sorry for what happened to your daughter. Losing her husband and child... my gosh I don't think I could survive it. How is Aaliyah?"

"She's getting better. Aaliyah's been staying with us, at our estate in New Jersey. She's barely left the house since I brought her back from Miami," Precious said, establishing an alibi for her daughter, just in case one is needed.

"That's wonderful. Right now she needs her family more than ever."

"Yes, family is so important, Chantal. That's why, while both of our daughters are going through such a difficult time, we have to remain united. We've had our differences and unfortunately Aaliyah and Justina aren't on speaking terms right now but we have to set a good example for them. Show them the importance of sticking together."

"Those are words I never thought I'd hear come out your mouth. I mean neither of us are saints, we're both much better sinners," Chantal giggled. "I think that's why we've never gotten along. We're too much alike. But I'll admit, I'm enjoying this female bonding and I genuinely appreciate your concern for Justina."

"To new beginnings and new friendships." Precious raised her glass and finished off the remainder of her wine. "I would love to stay, as I could chat with you all day but wife and mother duties call. Please keep me abreast of what's happening with Justina and your sweet grandbaby. I'm always here if you need someone to talk to." Precious gave Chantal a warm hug.

Precious went from sitting on a couch in Chantal's living room, to getting on her cell phone, the moment her heels touched the cement of the upper east side street.

"Hi Carlos, it's me Precious Mills."

"Good afternoon, Mrs. Mills, how are you?"

"I'm good and you?"

"Feeling great! Are you calling to let us know you'll be using the jet?"

"No, I was hoping you could help me with something else."

"I'll do my best, what do you need?"

"You know my daughter Aaliyah."

"Of course I know Miss Aaliyah."

Do you know the last time she used the

private jet?"

"Let me check the books. Just a moment," Carlos said putting Precious on a brief hold. "Nothing this year, Mrs. Mills. I'm not showing anything since Christmas."

"Really." Precious briefly felt a sigh of relief but she had to be sure. "Can you check and see if anyone used the jet on July 11th."

"Sure. Yes someone did use the jet."

"Who?"

"That's strange, a name wasn't written down. It just says female passenger with child."

"Thanks, Carlos. I appreciate your assistance."

"Of course, Mrs. Mills. Anytime. Make sure you tell your husband I said hello."

"Will do." Precious hung up with Carlos and wasted no time calling her daughter. Not surprisingly Aaliyah didn't answer her phone. "Aaliyah, this is your mother but you already know that! You better call me the moment you get this message. I'm on my way over right now. We need to talk!"

Precious had pulled her fair share of stunts in her life but kidnapping another woman's child was even too much for her to fully grasp. She didn't want to believe her daughter had gone completely over the edge but there weren't that many coincidences in the world. Regardless of her daughter's guilt, Precious was a mother first and she would do everything humanly possible to protect Aaliyah, even if it meant befriending Chantal.

$$$

"Omigoodness! Genesis, you're home!" Talisa ran towards her husband, clutching him tightly. "Where have you been?"

"It's a long story but I don't want to talk about any of that right now. I just want to hold my wife and my daughter. Where's Genevieve?"

"I put her down to sleep about an hour ago. She's missed you so much and so have I."

"Who are you in there talking to?" Amir called out to his mother, coming out the kitchen. "Dad, it's you! We thought you were dead." Amir went over to his father and held him tightly.

"I'm sorry but I needed for Arnez to believe I was dead. I needed all of you to react as if it was because I knew he would be watching," Genesis explained.

"Dad, Caleb has been working with Arnez! He played me. He played all of us. He's a snake just like Arnez. I thought Caleb had killed you."

"I know all about Caleb's relationship with Arnez," Genesis revealed.

"What...how?" Amir felt like the room was starting to spin.

"Caleb came clean with me about everything."

"When?"

"The night I went missing. When I told your mother I was meeting with him to discuss business."

"What! I thought that was the night Caleb probably killed you," Amir said, shaking his head.

"Again, that's what we wanted Arnez to believe. But we don't have to worry about Arnez ever again," Genesis said confidently.

"Why...what did you do?" Talisa wanted to know.

"Arnez is now deceased and he's really dead this time. I made sure to check his pulse, to remove any doubt," Genesis stated proudly.

"Thank goodness that man can never harm this family again," Talisa said, singing her husband praises.

"I don't understand any of this." Amir seemed flustered.

"Amir, how did you find out about Caleb's

dealings with Arnez?" Genesis asked.

"Arnez called and told me."

"When?"

"Earlier today. He was bragging, saying how Caleb had been working for him all this time and he gave the order for him to kill you. It made sense because you were missing and Caleb was missing too. How was we supposed to know, you and Caleb were working together." Amir looked defeated. "Now Caleb is probably dead because of me."

"Amir, you're not making sense right now," Genesis said.

"After I got the call from Arnez, I got everybody together and told them about the phone call. It took some time but we finally found the spot Caleb was hiding out at in the Bronx. Nico, Lorenzo and Supreme went there to deal with Caleb. They told me to stay here with Mom and Genevieve. I'm sure they went in asking no questions, just spraying bullets," Amir sighed.

"Caleb isn't in the Bronx and he was never there. By now he's probably halfway to Philly," Genesis told his son.

"Are you sure?"

"Positive."

"Then that's a good thing. It means Supreme

and them didn't have a chance to kill him."

"Don't you get it, Caleb was never there. Arnez purposely put that bullshit in your head."

"But why?"

"Oh shit...we gotta go. Call them and don't stop calling until one of them picks up!" Genesis yelled.

"Dad, what's going on?!"

"It's a trap. Not for Caleb but us. Arnez thought Caleb had killed me. Once he figured I was dead, it was about making sure the rest of you were dead too. What better way to do that than sending you all to hunt down the person you believed was responsible for murdering me."

"But Arnez is dead. He's no longer a threat," Talisa said confused.

"Yeah Arnez is dead but Maverick's not. Before he died, Arnez said Maverick would pick up where he left off. Now it all makes sense. We gotta go."

"Genesis, please be careful, you too Amir!" Talisa cried out.

"Dad, none of them are answering their phone."

"Keep calling!" Genesis's voice roared through the building. "Those are my brothas. If they die, the streets is done."

Read The Entire Bitch Series in This Order

Bitch
Joy Deja King
Bitch
Joy Deja King
Bitch Back
Joy Deja King
Queen
Joy Deja King
Last Bitch Standing
Joy Deja King
joy king
DIRTY LITTLE SECRETS
Joy King
hooker to housewife
Superstar
Joy Deja King
PAPER
Joy Deja King
Trife Life Lavish
Joy Deja King
PAPER II
Joy Deja King
PAPER
Joy Deja King
PAPER
Joy Deja King
PAPER
Joy Deja King
Trife Life Lavish Part 2
Joy Deja King
Rich Famous
Joy Deja King
Rich Famous
Joy Deja King
Famous
Joy Deja King
Bitch
Joy Deja King
Boss Bitch
Joy Deja King
Bitch
Joy Deja King
Bad Bitch
Bitch
Joy Deja King
Bitch
Joy Deja King
MAFIA Princess
Joy Deja King
MAFIA
Joy Deja King
MAFIA Princess
Joy Deja King
Chris Booker
MAFIA Princess
Joy Deja King
Chris Booker
MAFIA Princess
Joy Deja King
Chris Booker
Baller Bitches Volume 1
Joy Deja King
Baller Bitches Volume 2
Joy Deja King
Baller Bitches Volume 3
Joy Deja King
Baller Bitches The Reunion
Joy Deja King
Power
Joy Deja King
Power 2
Joy Deja King
DRAKE
Joy Deja King
Chris Booker
DRAKE II
Joy Deja King
Chris Booker
Ride Wit' Me
Joy Deja King
Ride Wit' Me 2
Joy Deja King
Hustler
Female Hustler
Joy Deja King
Female Hustler 3
Joy Deja King
Hustler 5
Joy Deja King
Hustler
Joy Deja King
Joy Deja King
Lovin' Enemy
Supreme
Joy Deja King
Joy Deja King
The Legacy
Joy Deja King
The Legacy Part II
Joy Deja King
ASSASSINS
Joy Deja King
ASSASSINS
Joy Deja King
ASSASSINS
Joy Deja King
Peter Mack
Joy Deja King
Peter Mack

A KING PRODUCTION
All I See Is The Money...
Female Hustler
A Novel
JOY DEJA KING

Prologue

Nico Carter

"I don't know what you want me to say. I do care about you—"

"But you're still in love with Precious," Lisa said, cutting me off. "I can't deal with this anymore. You're still holding a torch for a woman that has moved on with her life."

"Of course I have love for Precious. We have history and we share a daughter together, but I want to try and make things work with you."

"Oh really, is it because you know Precious has no intentions of leaving her husband or is it because of the baby?"

"Why are you doing this?" I shrugged.

"Doing what... having a real conversation with you? I don't want to be your second choice, or for you to settle for me because of a baby. Nobody even knows about me. I'm a secret. You keep our relationship hidden like you're ashamed of me or something."

"I'm not ashamed of you. With the business I'm in and the lifestyle I'm in, I try to keep my personal life private. I don't want to make you a target."

"Whatever. I used to believe your excuses, but my eyes have been opened. I'm a lot wiser now. I've played my position for so long, believing that my loyalty would prove I was worthy of your love, but I'm done."

"Lisa stop. Why are you crying," I said, reaching for her hand, but she pulled away. "I was always upfront with you. I never sold you a dream."

"You're right. I sold myself a dream. More like a fairytale. But when I heard you on the phone with Precious that fairytale died and reality kicked in."

"What phone conversation?" I asked, hoping Lisa was bluffing.

"The one where you told Precious she and Aaliyah were the loves of your life and nothing would change that, not even the baby you were having with me. It was obvious that was the first time you had ever even mentioned my name to her."

"Lisa, it wasn't like that," I said, stroking my

hand over my face. "You didn't hear or understand the context of the entire conversation." I shook my head; hating Lisa ever heard any of that. "That conversation was over a week ago, why are you just now saying something?"

"Because there was nothing to say. I needed to hear you say those words. I knew what I had to do and I did it."

"So what, you're deciding you don't want to deal with me anymore? It's too late for that. We're having a baby together. You gonna have to deal with me whether you want to or not."

"That's not true."

"Listen, Lisa. I'm sorry you heard what I said to Precious. I know that had to hurt, but again I think you read too much into that. I do care about you."

"Just save it, Nico. You care about me like a puppy," Lisa said sarcastically.

"I get it. Your feelings are hurt and you don't want to have an intimate relationship with me any longer, I have to respect that. But that doesn't change the fact you're carrying my child and I will be playing an active role in their life so I don't want us to be on bad terms. I want to be here for you and our baby."

"You don't have to worry about that anymore. You're free to pursue Precious and not feel obligated to me."

"It's not an obligation. We made the baby together and we'll take care of our child together."

"Don't you get it, there is no baby."

"Excuse me? Are you saying you lied about being pregnant?"

"No, I was pregnant, but..."

"But what, you had a miscarriage?"

"No I had an abortion."

"You killed my child?"

"No, I aborted mine!"

"That was my child, too."

"Fuck you! Fuck you, Nico! You want to stand there and act like you gave a damn about our baby and me. You're such a hypocrite and a liar."

"You had no right to make a decision like that without discussing it with me."

"I had every right. I heard you on the phone confessing your love to another woman and the child you all share together. Making it seem like our baby and me was some unwanted burden. Well now you no longer have that burden. Any child I bring into this world deserves better than that."

"You killed my child because of a phone conversation you overheard. You make me sick. I think I actually hate you."

"Now you know how I feel because I hate you too," Lisa spit back with venom in her voice.

"You need to go before you meet the same demise as the baby you murdered."

"No worries, I have no intentions of staying. As a matter of fact, I came to say goodbye. I have no reason to stay in New York."

"You're leaving town?"

"Yes, for good. Like I said, there is nothing here for me. I don't want to be in the same city as you. It would be a constant reminder of all the time I wasted waiting for you," Lisa said, as a single tear trickled down her cheek. "Goodbye, Nico."

I watched with contempt and pain as Lisa walked out the door. I couldn't lie to myself. I almost understood why she chose not to keep our baby. I wasn't in love with Lisa and couldn't see me spending the rest of my life with her. The fucked up part was it had nothing to do with her. Lisa was a good girl, but she was right, my heart still belonged to Precious. But I still hated her for aborting our baby. I guess that made me a selfish man. I wanted Lisa to bless me with another child that I could be a father to, but have her accept that she would never have my heart.

At this moment, it was all insignificant. That chapter was now closed. Lisa was out of my life. In the process, she took our child with her and for that I would never forgive her.

Seven Months Later...

"Look at her, mommy, she is so beautiful," Lisa said, holding her newborn daughter in the hospital.

"She is beautiful," her mother said, nodding her head. "What are you going to name her?"

"Angel. She's my little Angel." Lisa smiled.

"That's a beautiful name and she is an angel," Lisa's mother said, admiring her granddaughter. "Lisa, are you okay?" she asked, noticing her daughter becoming pale with a pain stricken expression on her face.

"I'm getting a headache, but I'll be fine," Lisa said, trying to shake off the discomfort. "Can you hold Angel for a minute. I need to sit up and catch my breath," Lisa said, handing her baby to her mother.

"I would love to." Her mother smiled, gently rocking Angel.

"I feel a little nauseated," Lisa said, feeling hot.

"Do you want me to get the nurse?"

"No, just get me some water," Lisa said. Before Lisa's mother even had a chance to reach for a bottle of water, her daughter began to vomit. In a matter of seconds Lisa's arms and legs began jerking. Her entire body seemed to be having convulsions."

"Lisa... Lisa... what's the matter baby!" Lisa's mother said, her voice shaking, filled with fear. "Somebody get a doctor!" she screamed out, running to the door and holding her grandbaby close to her chest. "My daughter needs a doctor. She's sick! Somebody help her please!" she pleaded, yelling out as she held the door wide open.

"Ma'am, please step outside," a nurse said, rushing into Lisa's room with a couple of other nurses behind her and the doctor close behind.

Lisa's mother paced back and forth in front of her daughter's room for what seemed like an eternity. "It's gonna be okay, Angel. Your mother will be fine," she kept saying over and over again to her grandbaby. "You know they say babies are healing, and you healing your grandmother's soul right now," she said softly in Angel's ear.

"Ma'am."

"Yes… is my daughter okay?" she asked rushing towards the doctor.

"Ma'am, your daughter was unconscious then her heart stopped."

"What are you saying?" she questioned as her bottom lip began trembling.

"We did everything we could do, but your daughter didn't make it. I'm sorry."

"No! No! She's so young. She's just a baby herself. How did this happen?"

"I'm not sure, but we're going to do an autopsy. It will take a couple of weeks for the results to get back. It could be a placental abruption and amniotic fluid embolism, or a brain aneurysm, we don't know. Again, I'm sorry. Do you want us to contact the father of your granddaughter?" the doctor asked.

Lisa's mother gazed down at Angel, whose eyes were closed as she slept peacefully in her arms. "I don't know who Angel's father is. That information died with my daughter."

"I understand. Again, I'm sorry about your daughter. Let us know if there is anything we can do for you," the doctor said before walking off.

"I just want to see my daughter and tell her goodbye," she said walking into Lisa's room. "My sweet baby girl. You look so peaceful." Lisa's mother rubbed her hand across the side of her face. "Don't you worry. I promise I will take care of Angel. I will give her all the love I know you would have. Rest in peace baby girl."

A KING PRODUCTION
Bad Bitches Only
ASSASSINS...
EPISODE 1
(Be Careful With Me)
JOY DEJA KING

Chapter One

He Loves Me

Bailey strutted out the Hartsfield-Jackson Atlanta International Airport, in her strappy, four inch snake-skin shoes, wearing matte black wire frame square sunglas ses and a designer suit tailored to fit her size six frame perfectly. The brown beauty looked like she was a partner at a powerful law firm, when actually she was barely a second year law student. But school was the least of her worries. Bailey had other things on her mind, like the promise ring she was wearing. It cost more than some people's home. Don't get it confused, this wasn't a promise of sexual abstinence. This was a promise of marriage, from her boyfriend of five years, Dino Jacobs.

"Keera," I was just about to call you girl," Bailey said, getting in her car.

"I was shocked as shit when you answered. I was expecting to leave a voicemail. You said you was gonna be in some conferences all day," Keera replied.

"Girl, I was but I checked out early. I'm back in the A."

"You back in Atlanta?!" Keera questioned, sounding surprised.

"Yep. That's why I was calling you. So we could do drinks later on tonight at that spot we like." Baily was getting hyped, as she was dropping the top on her Lunar Blue Metallic E 400 Benz.

"Most definitely...so where you headed now."

"Where you think...home to my man! Stop playin'," Bailey laughed, getting on interstate 75.

"I know yo' boo, will be happy to see you."

"Yep and his ass gon' be surprised too. He thinks I'm coming back tomorrow night. But I missed my baby. Plus that conference was boring as hell. All them snobby ass lawyers was workin' my nerves."

"Get used to it, cause you about to be one," Keera reminded her.

"Yeah but only cause Dino insisted. You know

I wanted to attend beauty school. I love all things hair and makeup. I have zero interest in law. But that nigga the one paying for it, so it's whatever," Bailey smacked.

"Girl, don't be wasting that man money. You better get yo' law degree and handle them cases!" Keera giggled.

"Okaaaay!! I believe Dino just want me to be able to represent his ass, in case anything go down," Bailey snickered.

"Well, let me get off the phone so you can get home."

"Keera, I know how to talk and drive at the same damn time," she popped.

"I didn't say you didn't but umm I have a nail appointment. You know they be swamped on a Friday," Keera explained.

"True. Okay, go get yo' raggedy nails done," Bailey joked. "Call me later, so we can decide what time we meeting for drinks."

"Will do! Talk to you later on."

When Bailey got off the phone with Keera, she immediately started blasting some Cardi B. The music, mixed with the nice summer breeze blowing through her hair, had her feeling sexy. She began imagining the dick down she'd get from Dino, soon as she got home.

"Here I come baby," Bailey smiled, pulling in the driveway. She was practically skipping inside the house and up the stairs, giddy like a silly schoolgirl. You'd think hearing Silk's old school Freak Me, echoing down the hallway, in the middle of the afternoon, would've sent the alarm ringing in Bailey's head. Instead, it made her try to reach her man faster.

It wasn't until she got a few steps from the slightly ajar bedroom door, did her heart start racing. Next came the rapid breathing and finally came dread. You know the type of dread, that seems like it's worse than death but you don't know for sure because you've never actually died. It was all too much for Bailey. Her eyes were bleeding blood. She wanted to erase everything she just witnessed and rewind time.

I shoulda kept my ass in DC, she screamed to herself, heading back downstairs and leaving the house. Once outside, Bailey started to vomit in the bushes, until there was nothing left in her stomach.

www.ingramcontent.com/pod-product-compliance
Lightning Source LLC
Chambersburg PA
CBHW022143160726
48282CB00024B/177